☞ BERNICE BALCONEY TO AURELIA SIPES

Dearest,

All your efforts to reinstate me into the good graces of the women's community in Milwaukee have come to naught. I ignominiously blew my debut with a group of artists, known as the Salon des Muses, whose invitation was the first break I've gotten since being kicked out of the Amazon publishing collective for insisting that we collect something. I wish these groups wouldn't pick such tricky names for themselves; how was I to know that the salon isn't a beauty parlor and the collective not a collection agency?

Bernice

A Comedy in Letters

by Georgia Jo Ressmeyer

ISBN 0-934816-06-9

Library of Congress Catalog Number:

83-63264

This project is supported, in part, by a grant from the
Wisconsin Arts Board, with funds from the State of
Wisconsin and the National Endowment for the Arts.

Thanks to Word City: Chicago Print Center for access
to typesetting equipment.

LOGO AND COVER DESIGN BY CHRIS JOHNSON

Cover production by Nancy Poore

This book is for my
friends in Milwaukee,
especially
Karen A. Snider
and
Barbara Behm.

BERNICE: A COMEDY IN LETTERS

by Georgia Jo Ressmeyer

A few years ago I met Bernice Balconey at a costume party. She had sewn a clear plastic cover over her entire body. She professed to be angry that no one had recognized her as a new couch.

The second time I saw her was last week, when she paid me a visit in my study. She sat with her back to the window on an old trunk full of papers across from my desk. Actually, what she did most was fidget. She was constantly in motion, tugging at her wild blond curls, snapping suspenders, ranging with impatient hands through myriad pockets. Hers was a rattling presence.

Bernice was small in frame, with knobby knees, hazel eyes, and sharp features. She sported footgear of her own manufacture: lavender court-jester slippers, embellished with sequins and wings which drooped about her ankles. In addition, she was wearing baggy, powder-blue shorts; a lavender T-shirt; white kneesocks, suspenders, and gloves; and a purple pith helmet, slung across her back. She carried a walking stick, topped by the head of a gavel.

Rather abruptly, Bernice started shoving papers at me. These she dug out of a crisp, brown shopping bag at her feet. Most of them appeared to be letters, some crumpled with wear. On the top of the stack she slapped a fresher-looking sheaf entitled "Introduction by Bernice Balconey."

"This," she said, tapping the pile with one end of her mallet, "is what I have questions about."

Since it appeared that she had come for legal advice, I explained that as an Inactive member of the State Bar, I was not in a position to dispense it.

Bernice assured me that "illegal advice" would be all the better. She said that she already had an attorney, but that for reasons which would become clear later, she could not consult with her on this particular matter.

Suddenly, as if remembering something that would bring her intentions into focus, she nimbly extracted a business card from a slender billfold and handed it to me. The card bore the following inscription: "Bernice Balconey: Theatrical Producer, *Artiste*, and Amateur Orthopedic Surgeon."

I was about to question her on that when she announced: "I'd like to publish these papers. I think they might be morally uplifting, and, frankly, I could use the cash." She said the manuscript was an exposé of "the legal system, the church, parental interference, romantic love, feelings, poetry, and nature." She'd apparently decided that as a writer as well as a lawyer, I could help her transform injustice into lucre.

I promised to look over the letters and render a verdict. This I accomplished within a few days. In no uncertain terms, I warned Bernice that publication would once again land her on the wrong side of the Law and should therefore be avoided.

As it turned out, Bernice completely disregarded my caution. She did, however, consent to my writing this preface disclaiming responsibility for her decision. That done, I would only confess that since I have always relished reading other people's mail, I thoroughly enjoyed my romp through Bernice's papers.

> Georgia Ressmeyer
> Milwaukee, Wisconsin

☞ INTRODUCTION by Bernice Balconey

Bernice Balconey was born in the fifth grade. I had a different name before then, a slave-name you might call it. I can't remember what it was exactly. Tallulah Bankhead or Tonawanda Station or Grace Schultz, something like that.

One day in fifth grade I put my foot down: no more belonging to my parents and being shorter than everybody else. Both my teacher and a goody-goody classmate, Bernice Woodby, were absent from school that day. What happened was that I sat at Bernice's desk, to the delight of the other students, and vandalized her academic career. I argued boisterously on her behalf that the name "Milwaukee" came from a beer bottle the Indians had found. And the answer sheet for her I.Q. test soon resembled one of mine — a big smudge. Like me, for once, she was judged not to have an I.Q. (which was no big deal — you could always tell people you were "off the charts").

Despite being found out and punished, or perhaps because of it, I vowed never to relinquish the name Bernice. A few days later I added the rest: Balconey, pronounced Balco'ny (as in Coney Island), unless someone accidentally got it right the first time — for them I said it was Bal'cony (as in porch or veranda). Actually, I almost settled on Porch for a name, but then I decided I didn't want to be confused with a foreign car. Balconey, besides being alliterative, rhymed with Baloney and sounded sort of Italian, which I liked because it seemed passionate and romantic and far away. I'd always thought of myself as a hot-blooded kid trapped in a frigid culture.

Born in 1950, I spent most of my life in Milwaukee. I was, as popular parlance had it, a P.K. —

Preacher's Kid. Like most such families we lived inside a washing machine that had a giant porthole window. People were always inspecting us — to make sure that we wore underwear, I guess.

Somehow all the attention drove me silly. I began pressing my nose against the glass and making faces. Before long I was wearing costumes and disguises. My parents never understood why I couldn't just "be myself," by which they seemed to mean that I should smile shyly, curtsy, mouth some platitude, and then be whirled about and dashed on my head. Why, indeed.

What my parents failed to recognize was the inherent contradiction in most people's expectations of P.K.'s: we would either set a perfect example for other children or else succumb at a shockingly early age to booze and wanton sex. I myself resolved this conflict in the only sensible way; I changed my name and claimed to be adopted.

Recently I found the following composition from fifth grade. It shows a lot about my state of mind:

October 31, 1960

Dear Visitors from Outer Space:

Hello. This is from Bernice Balconey, grade five. Our teacher said to write a letter for the time capsule in the cornerstone of our new school. Maybe in a million years, some outer space creatures will find the letters. I am trying to write clearly so you can figure out our language without too much frrzmblip.

Our teacher Miss Huggings assigned us to write different things. My job is to write about splubrs.

A splubr is a group of creatures who live in the same giql. Usually there are two big shots in each splubr and two or more slaves who do all of the work. The slaves are little people from a different planet. The big people send the slaves to school to make them forget about their home planet. I will never forget. The home planet is called Zrkblat. Please take all the slaves back to Zrkblat. Thank you.

Bernice Balconey
Citizen of Zrkblat

The teacher's comment, which was almost as long as my composition, is also revealing:

"This letter shows a lot of imagination, but you did not follow my instructions. Please do it over. Next time write about what families are really like. Address your composition to school children, not 'Visitors from Outer Space.' I am counting on you to help make the fifth grade's contribution to the time capsule something of which we can all be proud.

"Also, if I have to tell you one more time not to use the made-up name Bernice Balconey, I am going to report you to the principal. You may talk to your parents about changing your name, but until it is legally changed, you must continue to use the one that appears on your birth certificate."

I was the youngest of five children, the runt of the litter, the black sheep, an "accident." I spent most of my time in the attic writing mystery stories, painting frescoes, and sewing costumes for myself. One time I even tried to keep a journal. Here is how it went:

January 1, 1961

Dear Diary:

Aunt Irene gave me this book for Christmas. She

says I should write down what happens every day. But I hate what happens every day! But I promised to at least try.

Today we didn't go to school because it is a holiday. I stayed up in the attic. I have a room in the attic I call my Opium Den. I read about it in a book. This morning at church I said to the ladies, "Excuse me, I must go to my Opium Den."

Then I wrote a mystery about a peg-leg horse named Qumquat. Qumquat goes looking for a Great White Quail. The Great White Quail who bit her leg off many many years before. And I stayed away from Mother because she has an ullser from worrying about me. And besides she wants to punish me for getting my dress caught in her typewriter when I tried to type some Bible passages on the inside for the test in Sunday School.

See? I told you I would hate this. I am going to change this book to a map book or something.

From,
Bernice Balconey

After fifth grade it was all downhill. I performed badly in school. I frittered away my time. I had difficulty holding down a job. I made a fool of myself over and over again in romantic love. I got in trouble with the Law. I was always out of money. In fact, things only started picking up a couple months ago, when I conceived the plan to write this book, or rather to publish my correspondence from a particularly trying autumn.

What follows is a collection of letters (and a few journal entries and miscellaneous writings) which passed between myself and various other beings. It chronicles a period during which I fell afoul of love, art, and Milwaukee's night parking regulations. The principals in the story are:

AURELIA SIPES, erstwhile friend and lover, who was the recipient of a number of these missives, as we attempted, over a distance of a thousand miles, to salvage our relationship. Although a poet of ecstatic visions, Aurelia is as wholesome as the Wisconsin farm she grew up on – a condition I long ago learned to forgive. Her hair is golden-red and wavy, her temperament distressingly trusting. We had been living and writing together for almost a year when she left me for New Hampshire to study poetry, commune with nature, and escape my "warped" perspective, as she had the nerve to call it.

LILY BARNSTRAW, my attorney, irrationally appointed herself my guardian angel when my parents, with whom she had been friends, retired and moved away a few years ago. Lily is 58 years old, only slightly graying and regal in bearing. During the course of this past autumn I came to appreciate that underneath her majestic formality she is generous, compassionate, and dedicated to Justice – qualities only rarely encountered among members of her profession. I am truly grateful for her help with several unpaid parking tickets (about which more later), even though her lack of confidence in my ability to represent myself did undermine our case.

THE (dis)HONORABLE REGINALD H. COLLINS, Traffic Court Judge, is an arrogant, vindictive fellow, whose greatest pleasure lies in ridiculing poor people who appear in his courtroom. Why he singled me out as a special target for his harassment I may never discover, except that it might have something to do with my refusing to grovel. Even now when I picture his beady green eyes and blotchy skin, when I remember that strand of oily, reddish-brown hair that he wears plastered across his scalp, when I recall his high-pitched, sarcastic, whining voice, I am overcome with an irresistible impulse to offend him back.

MY PARENTS are much easier to forgive, especially now that they've retired and moved to Long Island. It was from MY MOTHER that I inherited my lack of height, my hazel eyes, and my curly blond hair, though she keeps hers under stricter control. Other than Church and Family, her grand passions are for flowers and colors, which may account for my occasionally flamboyant taste in clothing. In my view she is overly patient and solicitous toward MY FATHER, the minister, who tends to be moody and demanding. He is lean, long-faced, and stooped, and spends much of his time folding, unfolding, and twisting his ears. Lately I've come to think I may have a lot more in common with him than I would ever have cared to admit.

My friend NORA BLEEBLE has short dark hair, an ample build, and a guilty smile. We've known each other since the first day of kindergarten, when we convinced the other kids that we were joined at the shoulder. She accompanies me on many of my adventures and has even been known, on occasions when it was important for me to make an impression, to dress in uniform and play the role of my chauffeur. I have no complaints about her. She may even help me type this.

A more recent friend is ROWENA JASPERS,

musician and painter, whom I got to know while most of the letters in this book were being written. Feisty, intensely energetic, Rowena moves and acts with impulsive grace. One of our favorite pastimes is to argue raucously in public places about which of us is the quieter, less disputatious person.

The action of this book starts on September 6, about a week after Aurelia Sipes flew off to New Hampshire for the fall semester. She left me in charge of our apartment, most of her possessions, and her two kittens. Later she had reason to doubt my fidelity as a steward. My affection, on the other hand, has remained more or less constant, though whether she deserves it is another question.

☞ BERNICE BALCONEY TO AURELIA SIPES

September 6

Dear Aurelia:

Tell me now—and be honest—is there really such a thing as "The Country"? And what is this "Nature" we've heard so much about? Someone once told me that in a natural setting, nature doesn't have any broken glass or asbestos or bits of string lying about. Can this be true? It sounds Idyllic—that is, until you stop to consider that nature is an open sewer where animals "come" and "go" as they please without even bothering to clean up behind themselves. In fact, I'm sure it's filthy and disgusting, and I can't imagine why anyone would want to Get Back to there.

Don't misunderstand me, Aurelia. I like grass and trees as much as the next person. It's just that I think the city improves on nature by adding the human dimension. Right alongside our grass we have poptops and candy wrappers and cigarette butts. Not only do we have trees, but we have trees with kites and kitestring and old sweaters stuck in them. In contrast, nature unadorned is cold and impersonal.

Aren't you a nervous wreck by now? Come home, Aurelia. Swallow your pride and admit that city living is all you've ever really wanted. We'll sit on the front porch and watch the neighbor kids scream at each other. We'll listen to the siren symphony and sniff the garbage bouquet. Meanwhile I am sending energy to help you endure what must be a shattering experience.

Milwaukee and I will welcome you home with open arms, oh prodigal daughter. We may even slay a fatted soyaburger.

Courage my dear!

Your faithful roommate,

Bernice Balconey, President
NATURE IS FOR THE BIRDS, INC.

P.S. Had to pawn your guitar but should have it back by the time you return.

September 9

My dear Bernice:

Please be advised that I have conveyed your apologies to Judge Collins, and he has agreed to set a new hearing date on your parking tickets. As I have stated before, I am not in the least optimistic that he will reduce the fine, especially given the little "row" you and he had at the last hearing.

I cannot emphasize strongly enough that the procedure to follow in the event that I am again detained in another courtroom is this: inform the judge politely of my whereabouts and explain that I am expected momentarily. Do not attempt to represent yourself! Perhaps your citing fabricated cases last time had the court fooled for a moment, but even Judge Collins knows that the U.S. Constitution does not have a 33rd Amendment. And whether it should is not a matter to be debated in a courtroom.

As I stated to you in our telephone conversation of September 3, you do indeed have a constitutional right to represent yourself. However, I thought we also agreed on that date that your chances would be improved by having a lawyer, and I am happy to represent you gratis. Pardon me if this seems rigid and unspontaneous, but I really do believe your life would proceed more smoothly if you confined yourself to writing and left your business and legal affairs to me.

Further, I would be remiss in my duty as your legal advisor if I did not also comment on your attire at the last hearing, which I found inappropriate to say the least. First, is it too much to ask that you not wear that pencil-through-the-head contraption next time? Contrary to your prediction, it did not make the judge more sympathetic to your case. In fact, he suggested to me yesterday that perhaps you don't belong on the streets at all. Second, since I am more than willing to lend you a pair of galoshes if it rains again on the court date, you may leave your swim fins at home. And third, even blue jeans would be preferable to your high school strapless prom dress, although a nice pantsuit, as I have said before, is considered proper courtroom attire.

In answer to your phone message of yesterday, no, the judge is not likely to be persuaded by free samples of your poetry, because: 1) to the best of my knowledge he is not a lesbian; 2) he exhibits no symptoms of being in the least erotic; and 3) he is not renowned as a patron of the arts. In fact, be prepared for a lecture to the effect that you should get a job like everyone else.

Please meet me in my office at 10 a.m. on October 12. That will give us an hour before the hearing to come to some sort of agreement on testimony and dress. I know you are opposed in principle to "pandering to patriarchal standards" as you say, but in this case, wouldn't you rather pander a little than spend six days in jail? Of course, I leave this question entirely to your discretion.

Thank you for the "Ode on a Lawyer's Office Door." If you do not see it there the next time you drop by, it is because, as I have remarked before, you are ahead of your time—not because I do not appreciate your work. Perhaps in another twenty years the rest of my clients will appreciate it, too.

I look forward to seeing you on October 12 at 10 a.m.

Yours sincerely,

Lily Barnstraw
Attorney at Law

☞ BERNICE BALCONEY TO LILY BARNSTRAW

September 13

My dear Ms. Barnstraw:

You will be pleased to learn that I have been availing myself of the facilities at the County Law Library to instruct myself further in the intricacies of our legal system. Rest assured that I have found numerous cases to support our position, and that I will bring them with me to court.

The most cogent, I think, is the case of Queen Elizabeth vs. William Shakespeare, in which the court found that "the playwright, for all he doth offend, doeth the crown proud." And lest you misdoubt the application of that historic precedent to my own self, please be advised that in the last day and a half I have been writing plays to beat the band (including, appropriately enough, a courtroom tragedy starring an elderly spinster lawyer fighting courageously against the forces of evil, as personified by a nasty traffic court judge. Sound familiar? Incidentally, the lawyer loses in the end because she is too proud to accept the advice of her wise, albeit youthful, client).

I will meet you in court at 10 a.m. on November 12, as per your epistle. And don't worry. If you're late, I know exactly what to do. In fact, I've prepared a little speech for just that eventuality: "Your Majesty, the *corpus delectable* of my esteemed attorney can be obtained by writ of *habeas corpus.* I, however, appear *in appropriate persona* and am prepared to proceed on the merits, *quid pro quo* and *sine qua non,* since *hunky dory* the facts speak for themselves. And if your royal highness is not totally won over by my arguments, I intend to take this case all the way to the Supreme Court, *semper paratus, e pluribus unum, ad infinitum,* and *sic transit gloria mundi.*"

That ought to do the trick. Don't you agree? By the way, I meant what I said about your *corpus* being *delectable.* Of course, that's pure speculation on my part and would probably be overruled in a court of law, but I have a certain "feel" for these things, and—believe me—the facts almost always bear me out.

I hope you made a copy of my "Ode on a Lawyer's Office Door" before you violated my constitutional right to free speech by obliterating it. I will have my lawyer contact you about this; perhaps some kind of settlement can be reached. If not, I have only one thing to say, and that is: "See you in court!"

Signed,
Your colleague of the
Bench and Bar,

Bernice Balconey
Esqueer

P.S. I am taking you up on your excellent suggestion that I stick to writing. In fact, I have just mailed a

very stirring letter to Judge Collins, which I am
confident will clinch our case for us.

☞ BERNICE BALCONEY TO JUDGE COLLINS

September 13

Dear Your Honor:

Have I unwittingly offended you? Please
understand that it was never my intention to
besmirch the somber dignity of the court. Anyone
can tell you I am totally awed by the majesty and
wisdom of your position. In fact, my knees quake at
the mere thought of your absolute sovereign
dominion over lowly parking violators like myself.

My attorney, Ms. Lily Barnstraw, informs me
that you were somewhat put off by my attire at the
last hearing. In light of your misapprehension, I
think it only fair to offer a word of explanation.

Judge Collins, surely you have heard of that
disgusting condition known as poverty. And
whatever your thoughts about poor people's lack of
motivation, you are no doubt also aware of the latest
research linking poverty to a virus that can only be
overcome by rubbing the infected area with hundred-
dollar bills. I mention this not as an argument in
favor of distributing free money to the poor —
although experts say that may become necessary to
stave off an epidemic — but as an argument against
wholesale condemnation of the indigent. After all,
they may have done nothing more to bring on their

poverty than spend too little time counting their money.

Unfortunately, I am a chronic sufferer from this disease, which accounts for my apparel at the last hearing. The pencil-through-the-head was all I had to keep the hair out of my eyes; the swim fins served in lieu of galoshes; and the dress I wore was the only item of clothing left after the rummage sale I was forced to conduct last week. So you see, I meant no disrespect.

Ms. Barnstraw also intimated you were unimpressed by my legal arguments. Although I still firmly believe that there ought to be a 33rd Amendment exempting artists from legal accountability for their actions, it was perhaps naive of me to assume that a traffic judge would keep abreast of the latest developments in civil libertarian theory. My apologies for presuming you would be familiar with the theoretical underpinnings of my argument.

As for getting a job, I would love to have one. In fact, I have been wondering for years what it must be like to have a job. Do you know of any openings at the courthouse? Although my training and experience best qualify me for work as a sort of roving *artiste*, I think I would also make an excellent judge. At least as a judge I wouldn't have to worry about my wardrobe; for all anyone knew I could be stark naked underneath my robes.

Which brings me to the naked truth — namely, that I am unable at this time to pay the $120 fine for my accumulated parking tickets. I realize that instead of the fine, you have generously offered to let me spend six days in jail. Quite frankly, I would prefer not to go to jail for such an unpoetic offense as parking on the street without a permit. Couldn't we change it to something more inspirational – like impersonating a jury or burning soft coal too near the Capitol? I try to find material for my writing in every experience I have, but my creativity balks at making something beautiful, or even interesting, out of going to jail for unpaid parking tickets.

Judge Collins, I would throw myself on the mercy of the court were I not fearful of spreading the infection. I beg you, do not deal harshly with me. The offending vehicle has long since been junked, and it is very rare these days for me to feel, let alone succumb to, the temptation to park illegally at night. Since I am almost completely rehabilitated, wouldn't the city benefit more by giving me a couple hundred dollars to rub on my poverty, or at least by convicting me of an offense that will boost my credibility and, therefore, marketability as an artist?

I know you are a fair man and will give these suggestions your careful consideration. Thanking you in advance for your cooperation.

                                  Respectfully submitted,

                                  Bernice Balconey
                                  Reformed Criminal

☞ AURELIA SIPES TO BERNICE BALCONEY

New Hampshire
September 15

Bernice, Bernice, Bernice:

i don't know what to say, my head is echoing. No, it is not marijuana, it is from living in the mountains. The mist that rises from the valleys, cascading water, animals leaping and dancing, flowers like precious jewels — here is my habitat.

And punctuation, Bernice, today i think punctuation is to help city people keep their minds off ugliness. My poetry instructor Jenny Fribbenz keeps reminding me that i will need to remember the rules when my money runs out i will find an employer who cares i am a bird i am a deer i am a cotton-tail my spirit is unleashed i have never felt so happy or so free.

u are always making fun of me Bernice but really u would love it here, u are wrong to be suspicious, u are simply afraid to try it. i wish u would come out here to visit.

But oh u know the rules would have to be different, i couldn't stand to have u mocking everything, u would have to learn to relax and enjoy and receive instead of trying to impose your weird sense of disorder on the world. u are not the center of the universe, u know, we are all but single cells in a vast creation — the Goddess or however we choose to call it. But here i go preaching again.

It is something of a catharsis to be able to write this to u. i guess that is the value of physical distance, i don't really care if u think i am sentimental or silly.

The point is i am happy. i want u to be happy too.
Love,

Aurelia

☞ BERNICE BALCONEY TO AURELIA SIPES

September 20

Dear Aurelia:

Ewe are right about punctuation. Eye tried to write a whole letter in run-on sentences (after performing warm-up exercises that included leaping about the room in the manner of a deer frolicking in the early morning mist), but as Eye wrote Eye became increasingly weighted down by the ugliness of the urban environment. It was not until Eye retreated again to the prosaic world of periods and commas that the gloom began to lift. Thank the Goddess, of whom Eye am but a single cell, for inventing rules of grammar as a salve for us city-dwellers. There have to be some compensations.

Oh, Aurelia, I can't believe you are actually falling for all that Beauty-of-Nature garbage. Can't you see that it's just a lot of tinsel and glitter designed by some cynical exterior decorator to keep our minds off human suffering? Nature was created purely for escapist entertainment, like a pleasure park at an imperial palace. Reality, Aurelia, is an old shoe with a hole in its sole. Reality is how you make me suffer.

Meanwhile, your kittens are driving me crazy.

Prufrock bites me every time I say anything in the least derogatory about poets or poetry, and Ariel just survived her fifteenth suicide attempt. Couldn't you have given them normal names, such as Margaret Mead or Simone de Beauvoir? More important, who is going to pay for the little magazines they keep ordering?

Aurelia, if you don't come home soon I may decide to join Ariel in her next leap into the toilet. Then who will keep you filled in on the "haps" in Cream City? Think about it.

                              Signed,
                              Your Penpal,

                              Bernice Balconey
                              Native of the Urban Blight

P.S. Had to pawn your stereo but should have it back by the time you return.

☞ BERNICE BALCONEY TO HER PARENTS (UNSENT)

                              September 23

Dear Mom and Dad,

I bet by now you are wondering what ever happened to your favorite daughter. I tried calling you a few times, but, unfortunately, my phone's been disconnected and nothing happens when I dial. Oh well, it's the thought that counts, right?

Gosh, I miss you two. Did you get the flowers I

sent for Mother's Day and Father's Day? Quite frankly, I'm suspicious of the man at the florist's. He looks like the type who would take your money but never follow through. That may be why you didn't get them – assuming you didn't get them, of course.

Maybe you did get them. Maybe he had a pang of remorse and sent them after all, if he hadn't lost your address by then. The whole thing makes me so angry I could scream. My only consolation is in knowing that at least you got the cards – that is, unless the rumor is true about the weird man at the post office who rips up greeting cards. (It's a tragic case: both of his parents died from paper-cut infections after a rush Christmas-card job. Folks say he's never been quite "right" since.)

In answer to the only letter of yours that I could find (sorry about that – I wonder what could have happened to the rest?):

1.) The reason Pastor Gunderson doesn't know who I am is because I'm always too busy after church straightening the pews, picking up bulletins, and replacing hymnals in their holders to join the receiving line in the narthex. I don't mind effacing myself, like the Suffering Servant, in the performance of these humble chores, except that now you think that I must not be going to church. Oh, ye of little faith. . .

2.) I broke off my relationship with that "nice young man" you asked about. It seems he believes in pre-marital sex, which I am dead set against. Although in these days of moral decadence it may be difficult, if not impossible, to find a man of like moral fiber to myself, I am determined to hold out until I do – even if that means remaining a spinster all my life. No one will ever convince me that sexual fulfillment and grandchildren are as important as sticking to what I know is right.

3.) I have no idea how Aurelia is. She's been out of town for almost a month, and I'm horny as heck.

Well, got to run. Although you didn't ask about my finances, I'm sure you meant to. Actually, they're terrible, but please don't worry about me! Eventually I'll be able to buy back all the stuff I pawned, including Grandma's favorite brooch. And Aunt Clarissa has me over for dinner once a month, so I am eating. In short, all is well with your devoted daughter.

> A thousand kisses to my
> darling parents,
> Signed
>
> Bernice Balconey
> Perfectly Pious Progeny

☞ BERNICE BALCONEY TO HER PARENTS (SENT)

September 23

Dear Mom and Dad,

When Mother's Day slipped by me without warning, I determined to honor both of you on Father's Day. Unfortunately, now that you've retired and moved away, those exquisite funeral-home calendars are no longer available to me; in consequence, I never know what day it is. Can you forgive me for being so inattentive to High Holy Days like the above?

All's well here in Milwaukee. Aurelia, I think I told you, is in New Hampshire for the fall semester. This apartment is so quiet I can barely not hear myself think.

Got to run. Sorry this is so short. I just wanted to let you know I'm grateful to you for bringing me into this world and for not abandoning me on someone else's doorstep until I survived the formative years – my early twenties.

I hope you are well and enjoying your solitude.

Love,

Bernice

☞ JOURNAL ENTRY BY BERNICE BALCONEY

September 24

Dear Diary,

You may wonder what is on the outside of these two covers. More particularly, how are you dressed, what is your usual place of habitation, and, finally, which world, which galaxy, which universe must you traverse? Are you my slave or are we equaller than that? Do I write to you or merely through you to someone else?

I wonder: am I an animist? Do you have a spirit? Is there such a thing as reincarnation? Have you been a diary in previous lives, or are diaries immortal? Do I create you, or is it vice versa? Why am I asking so many questions?

This much I can tell you: I bought you in a store for $2.03, tax included. You were not my first choice. What I really wanted — as soon as I set eyes on her, that is — was a large, heavy, official-looking tome of the kind that judges' clerks write in. That would have cost me $18.95 plus tax, or —
viewing it another way — about two weeks groceries. I opted for survival and came home with you.

There were two reasons for choosing you over several similarly-priced models, both of them having to do with your inspirational properties. First, you are red, which stirs me to passion. And second, you bear on your front as well as on your spine a single word, a simple yet profound admonition: "Record." I shall try to live up to that command, since it may well be the only direct communication I receive from you.

I am convinced that you have your own separate existence, your own mysterious characteristics, your own rules of behavior. It seems not unlikely that you descend from a powerful race of diaries that has attracted and enslaved millions of followers over the centuries. Doubtless you are as eager to make a junkie out of me as I am to understand your secrets. Am I right? Are you sure you want to take me on? See you soon.

Bernice

September 27

To the Women of the Salon des Muses:

It is with a certain amount of embarrassment that I am writing to you. I fear that my behavior at your Saturday afternoon meeting was alienating in the extreme. For the disruption I caused, you have my apologies. Although I despair of regaining your respect and know that your doors may be forever shut to me, I feel in my heart that I owe you some kind of explanation.

When I received your invitation in the mail I was flattered and excited. The quality of the artwork made it clear that the group for which it spoke aspired to excellence, a virtue I admire from afar. I resolved to attend your gathering even though it meant missing my yodeling lesson.

Where I went awry was in my reading of your invitation, which I think you will admit required some patience to decipher. In my excitement over the design, I made a silly and perhaps unpardonable mistake: in place of the word "salon" I saw "saloon." Quite frankly, from the name of your group as it appeared to me—the Saloon des Muses—I inferred that you were opening a new women's bar, whose birth I was invited to celebrate. It did not occur to me that you were holding regular receptions to discuss artistic and literary issues. I assure you that I would not have come pretending to be drunk had I known that my condition would be remarked upon unfavorably. I was trying to fit in.

You may wonder at my behavior upon walking into a room of serious faces in which a discussion of feminism and art appeared to be taking place. I hope you will believe that I did not at once discover my mistake. In fact, my impulse was to sacrifice my own reputation as a dignified proponent of the arts in order to add a little life to a party I thought was bombing miserably. Why else would I have leapt up on a table and shouted "Let's boogie." Or, when that failed to rouse the crowd, why would I have said "Come on, sisters! I can't believe all these glum faces! What do you think this is — a poetry reading?"

Well, as I found out later, it was a poetry reading, and now all the poets in the group are angry with me. Sisters, the last thing I wanted to do was give you the impression that I have something against poetry. The truth is, I love poetry. It's just that sometimes when I hear a voice somberly intoning to a worshipful audience, I get confused and think I am in church, which triggers images of crucifixions and crowns of thorns and ears being cut off by irate disciples or painters. I have a tendency in such moments to become lewd and start orgies.

To prove to you that I meant no disrespect, that I am, in fact, in total agreement with your goals, I would like to donate to your organization, free of charge, a can't-miss, money-making idea that has the potential not only to fund your activities but also to spread feminist culture to the masses. All I ask in return is your attention while I set forth the philosophy behind my invention.

Did any of you as children mess around with those tacky paint-by-numbers sets? If so, you'll recall that the only way to have any fun with them was to disregard the lines and numbers, yet to make the picture look authentic by covering the entire surface

with tiny, indiscriminate globs of paint. The capper
was to present the completed masterpiece to
whichever aunt gave you the kit in the first place,
insisting that the perfect spot for it is over the
fireplace where Great-grandfather Helmut used to
hang. Naturally, a budding artist like yourself would
also want to visit the painting at least once a day
until the following Christmas — when you might be
surprised to receive cash from your aunt instead of
the candle-making kit you kept hinting you wanted.

The most objectionable feature of those paint-by-
numbers sets is that they do not leave room for
creativity. While the goal of spreading art to the
masses is admirable, the approach of the paint-by-
number moguls is far too limited: they treat people
as mindless automatons who are incapable of
contributing anything of their own to the art-making
process. My suggested improvement to the concept
would treat people as mindless automatons whose
lapses of taste and coordination should be
incorporated in some positive and constructive way.

Actually, I think the paint-by-numbers market
is probably saturated. I suggest that instead you work
up a whole line of poetry-by-numbers kits. Not only
does this plan have the potential to de-mystify poetry
for the masses, but it might also de-mystify wealth
for your organization.

To give an example of how the idea might be
carried out, take the following poem by Emily
Dickinson:

> There is no frigate like a book
>   To take us lands away,
> Nor any coursers like a page
>   Of prancing poetry —

This traverse may the poorest take
Without oppress of toll —
How frugal is the chariot
That bears a human soul!

Before being filled in, a typical poetry-by-numbers parchment might look like this:

There is no ___(1)___ like a ___(2)___
To ___(3)___ us ___(4)___ away,
Nor any ___(5)___ like a ___(2)___
Of ___(6)___ ___(7)___ —

This traverse may the ___(6)___ est ___(3)___
Without oppress of ___(2)___ —
How ___(6)___ is the ___(1)___
That ___(3)___ a human ___(8)___ !

A possible number key reads as follows:

(1) type of vehicle
(2) singular noun
(3) verb
(4) plural noun
(5) type of animal
(6) adjective
(7) type of literature
(8) part of the body

And finally, here is an example of how a poet-by-numbers might complete the poem:

There is no auto like a porche
To whisk us worlds away,
Nor any weasel like a mink
Of gaudy poesy —

> This traverse may the richest ride
> Without oppress of rancor –
> How maddening is the pogo stick
> That jolts a human ankle.

Who's to say that isn't an improvement on Dickinson?
Certainly not me.

My best wishes for the continued success of your
project. Perhaps someday I will live down my
reputation as a rabble-rouser and be accepted into
the arms of my sisters – which, believe me, is where
I long to be.

>> Penitentially yours,

>> Bernice Balconey

☞ BERNICE BALCONEY TO AURELIA SIPES

>> September 29

Dearest,

All your efforts to reinstate me into the good
graces of the women's community in Milwaukee
have come to naught. I ignominiously blew my debut
with a group of artists, known as the Salon des Muses,
whose invitation was the first break I've gotten since
being kicked out of the *Amazon* publishing collective
for insisting that we collect something. I wish these
groups wouldn't pick such tricky names for
themselves; how was I to know that the salon isn't a
beauty parlor and the collective not a collection
agency? It seems I have more trouble than most

people with Words. Right now I'm endeavoring to eliminate them from my vocabulary.

I won't bore you with pleas to come home. It's enough that you know my life has disintegrated completely since your departure: everything I own is pawned; I haven't eaten for days; the love of my life is cavorting naked in the woods a thousand miles away; and other women keep throwing themselves at my body.

Oh, Aurelia, I'm confused. Of course I remember every detail about our life together, but could you tell me once more how much you paid for that sewing machine?

Your mother called again last Thursday night. I told her you were washing your feet and couldn't come to the phone. The time before that I said you were cutting your toe-nails. She's starting to think you have a foot-fetish. If you don't send new excuses soon, I may break down and tell her the truth — that you're pregnant and too embarrassed to talk with her. Besides the above, here are some I've already used: you just stepped out to make a phone call; you're in church; you're helping a boy scout cross the street; and you're cleaning out the chimney. (Sorry about the latter — I panicked. She asked if that isn't the landlord's responsibility; I said he gives us a break on the rent, etc., etc.)

Well, got to run. There's a woman coming over who promised to give me a postage stamp in exchange for some as-yet-unspecified service. I wonder what it is.

Almost all my love —

Bernice

P.S. Had to pawn your sewing machine but should have it back by the time you return.

P.P.S. As per your advice of this summer, I think I will apply to the Wisconsin Arts Conclave for a grant in creative writing. Their next deadline is October 1, which means I have two whole days to put something together. Are you proud of me for planning ahead?

☞ BERNICE BALCONEY TO THE WISCONSIN ARTS CONCLAVE

October 1

Dear Wisconsin Arts Conclave:

In the past few weeks you have undoubtedly read so many neatly typed, perfectly structured, and energetically expounded grant proposals that you will have little tolerance for a hand-scrawled letter of the kind you now see before you. In fact, you may wonder why read this at all when so many deserving artists have demonstrated far greater discipline and apparent zeal in tackling the application process. In consequence of my relatively weak position vis-à-vis your guidelines, I have decided upon a policy of complete honesty and directness; rather than grovel or cajole, let me say simply, and with humility, that the Environment I wish to construct — entitled WHAT LESBIANS DO — is the sort of project the Wisconsin Arts Conclave would want to encourage and to subsidize.

Although, personally, I regard as inexcusable

my failure to submit this request on the standard application form, various friends have urged me to reconstruct for you the extenuating circumstances that kept me from paying my usual obeisance to bureaucratic necessity. Some of these friends are themselves former grant recipients. They assured me that the members of the Wisconsin Arts Conclave are so sympathetic to struggling artists that a refusal on my part to explain the difficulties I experienced would insult both your sensitivity and your generosity — which, I assure you, is not my intention.

It may come as a surprise to learn that this very morning I held in my hand a beautifully typed and compellingly expressed grant proposal, written and illustrated by me for submission to the Wisconsin Arts Conclave. My friends had been so impressed by my final draft that one of them offered to type the proposal free of charge. Unfortunately, this plan necessitated my walking more than six miles to pick up the completed manuscript, since I was without either vehicle or bus fare.

As so often happens to the impecunious when attempting to pull ourselves up by our own bootstraps, my foot slipped — to be precise, on the Sixteenth Street viaduct while crossing the Industrial Valley. The papers were sent whistling, tearing, and flapping across freight yards and factory roofs by an awesome wind which I could not help thinking was sent to test my devotion to Art. Quite frankly, fellow practitioners, I cried; to see all existing copies of the labor of love that had been my grant proposal scattered irretrievably across that vast, polluted canyon broke my heart — but not, I am happy to report, my spirit.

In the few moments that remain before I must mail this letter to insure that it is properly postmarked, I shall attempt to describe the project I hope to undertake with your assistance. My plan, briefly stated, is to construct an entire room, or Environment, around the theme of WHAT LESBIANS DO. The top half of the door leading into the room, which will remain locked at all times, will contain a window large enough to permit two or three people to view the goings-on inside. Some of the space around the lower half of the door will be occupied by a dummy of Anita Bryant's husband, peeking through the keyhole. The viewers who share this floor space with the dummy will have the option to sit or lean on him, depending, of course, upon their own sexual preference and how tired they become.

Time does not permit me to describe the inside of the Environment in detail. I would like to point out, however, that I will research the topic exhaustively and that my representation will be both realistic and artistically innovative. Until I am able to interest a museum in purchasing this Environment, I plan to set it up in my bedroom. Needless to say, the members of the Wisconsin Arts Conclave will be invited to a preview showing.

The postal clerk is signalling that my time is almost up, so I will sign off by saying Thank You for your kind attention.

Respectfully submitted,

Bernice Balconey
Visual Artist

P.S. [hastily scrawled on the envelope] I am asking
for $5,000 — a paltry sum considering the vast
number of moving parts, countless hours of tedious
research, and the profound social significance of a
work of this kind. I would settle for $3,000, however,
if you're really in a pinch. Once again, thank you. B.B.

☞ HER MOTHER TO BERNICE BALCONEY

Long Island
October 2

Dear Bernice:

Your Father and I are off to the Graebers for
cocktails any minute, so this will have to be short.

We had a very nice Father's Day. Madge, Steve,
and the kids came down from Connecticut, and all
the others (with one exception, ahem) called. When
are you getting a telephone? The only one your Father
didn't hear from was you, and naturally he was a
little bit perturbed — not for himself, of course, but in
case you might be in some kind of trouble. Your letter
was a slight consolation. Even though it came very
very late, you at least remembered to mention
Father's Day. I hope you know *I* don't care about
cards and presents and all that brouhaha, but your
Father, who would never admit this, is really very
sensitive. Well, 'nuf said. Please don't forget his
birthday, which is December 1 — exactly three weeks
after mine, if that helps you to remember it (but don't
worry about me — I've never cared for birthdays, as

you well know).

Your Father and I were talking about you last night, which we do often. Because he cares so very much about you, he is a little bit concerned about whether you are spending enough time trying to make new friends. I can't help remembering when you were young and used to lock yourself in the attic for hours and sew buttons all over your clothes, or something, instead of playing with the other children. I don't pretend to understand or judge the way you live, but your Father worries sometimes that you don't get out enough. Nothing against Aurelia, who seems like a lovely person, but isn't your world a little too narrow when you only spend time with her and a few other female liberationists? Don't forget there are men out there and plenty of nice ones like your Father who will try to give you *space* to be somewhat independent. Of course, it's your life and I am only passing on some of your Father's concerns, which he might not get around to telling you himself. 'Nuf said.

Well, your Father is up from his nap, so I'd better hurry and get ready — you know how impatient he gets.

Write soon.

                    Love,

                    Me

P.S. After the Cocktail Party: Do you remember Annie Graeber? Her husband, age 30, is now some kind of big wheel on Wall Street. They have three adorable children. She asked how you are doing. It's always so hard to know what to answer, since you never tell us anything. (Hint, hint)

P.P.S. Your Father sends his love. He says to
convey his greetings to Pastor Gunderson next
Sunday — if you're going to Church, that is.

P.P.P.S. We pray for you every night.

☞ AURELIA SIPES TO BERNICE BALCONEY

New Hampshire
October 4

Bernice:

Irrational joy — that first gust of snow, and I
remember how we used to go to Big Bay Park to
celebrate our changing expectations. Jill Frost, we
said, will soon arrive, with her palette of crystal and
her naturalist's eye, her delicate brushes, her lacy
style, her hardy constitution. Now she shocks us
with her boldness, now she makes us sigh, now we
gape in wonder — each canvas, each window a
panoramic scene, or else a microcosm.

Sometimes in anger, next in sheer elation, she
paints her moods; she draws our spirits to the
window and she traces us — then, ill-tempered, blows
a frigid blast to freeze us in our tracks, or else with
gentle breath seduces us to linger for the sunrise.

Have i told you about my teacher Jenny Fribbenz?
Oh Bernice i think u would like her, she has sad brown
eyes, a liquid voice, and beautiful broad shoulders —
and she writes with such lyrical intensity! How she
must suffer!

Oh i know u always say suffering is a waste of
time Bernice but in this case she doesn't seem to
have much choice, i mean apparently her life has
been a series of tragic events. And though it may be
understandable for someone like u — whose torments
are usually self-inflicted — to dismiss all tragedy as
self-indulgence, this woman has experienced a lot,
Bernice. i mean she has probably had more misery
than any ten people, the kinds of things u probably
think only happen in novels. Anyway when i start to
think about what sheltered lives both u and i have
had, i'm glad to be finally branching out into the real
world.

i know you keep wishing i'll come right home
but maybe instead if u think about me coming home
older and wiser u'll get used to the idea of waiting a
little longer. Maybe u'll end up liking me better, maybe
there will be less to make fun of. i sincerely do hope
that happens.

        Love,

        Aurelia

☞ JOURNAL ENTRY BY BERNICE BALCONEY

        October 8

Suicide. Today someone asked me if I believed in
it. "Only when the decision is unanimous," I said,
walking away. Pressed to elaborate, I added: "The
word suicide comes from the Latin, meaning 'at the

side of Suey.' Scholars differ as to whether that refers to a person named Suey or a hog call. In either case, it doesn't sound very appealing."

☞ BERNICE BALCONEY TO AURELIA SIPES

October 8

Dear Aurelia:

Why didn't you tell me there's such a thing as "Non-Monogamy?" I always knew people cheated on their lovers, but I never knew there was a whole philosophical system to support that practice. Needless to say, my head is reeling with the implications. And to make the mental adjustment from thinking that infidelity is responsible for the downfall of Western Civilization to thinking that loving more than one person at a time is the cutting edge of the Revolution — well, Aurelia, what can I say: it isn't easy but I'm putting heart, soul, and body into making the millennium. The Goddess knows I've never been one to shirk my responsibility to future generations.

I've been spending a little time lately with a woman named Rowena Jaspers, who used to play and sing with a band called The Joy of Hetero Sax. Shucks, Aurelia, no sense beating around the bush: she's moved into our apartment and is sleeping in my bed. Of course, this is only temporary. She's in the process of breaking up with her lover and needed a place to stay. Since I've finally stopped anticipating your imminent return, I figured I might as well get a little help with the rent. If you have any objections to this arrangement, please let me know by 6 p.m. today, which is when she's moving her baby grand into your bedroom. As for your bed, don't worry — I'll find a nook for it.

Space, as always, is problematic. It looks as though Rowena and I will have to share a bed until we figure out a better way to fit her four rooms of furniture into our two room apartment. Right now it's possible to go all the way from one end to the other without seeing, let alone touching, the floor. The place looks more like a furniture warehouse than Home Sweet Home. It's a good thing I'd already pawned most of our stuff.

To get back to Rowena for a minute: she's setting up a new, all-women's band called Circe and the Sirens. I've agreed to write lyrics for them. Most of the lyrics I'm working on have to do with you running off and leaving me high and dry.

Rowena keeps trying to cheer me up by telling me all about non-monogamy, and how if nobody thinks they own anybody else, and if everyone shares their favors with everyone else, then losing one lover to nature won't be the end of the world any more. What do you think? Should I investigate this further? Heck, if my sleeping around is going to prevent others from feeling hurt and abandoned like I did, don't I owe it to my sisters to give freely of myself? Row says definitely yes. Gee, she's unselfish. We're really starting to be close friends.

Write soon and tell me whether you agree that this non-monogamy business has a lot of potential.

Non-possessively yours,

Bernice Balconey

P.S. If you're sleeping with anyone else, I don't want to hear about it.

☞ BERNICE BALCONEY TO *AMAZON*

October 9

Dear *Amazon*:

I am submitting, for your consideration, what might appear to be no more than a dusty and dilapidated xerox machine. I urge you to examine my submission more carefully. In case the immortal lines I have etched in the dirt thereon have become blurred or obliterated, here is an exact transcription — affectionately titled "Ode on a Xerox Machine."

Copy Cat:

in the
pellucid
pre-cision
of your
process

take and make me into
something finer

Or,
if not finer
then more often,
for

in safety there is numbers
someone told me

      pass it
      on

Although, naturally, I would prefer that you published the entire work, I understand that the costs of duplicating and distributing a few thousand xerox machines may be prohibitive. If absolutely necessary, you have my permission to run a photographic reproduction of my poem instead. Please inform your readers that this gem is part of a collection of my poetry that I am assembling for publication in book form. I call it, appropriately, *Xerox Loving Xerox.* It is all about a woman's right to control her reproductive functions.

                    Duplicitously yours,

                    Bernice Balconey
                    Replica and/or
                    Facsimile

☞ BERNICE BALCONEY TO HER PARENTS (UNSENT)

                    October 12

Dear Mom and Dad:

What do you mean when you say my world is too "narrow?" Is Long Island situated on another planet? The fact is, I live in the same world I always have inhabited — and so, I suspect, do you. I don't recall seeing anything on T.V. about this problem. Are you privy to inside information you aren't telling me about? Please advise. Certainly the knowledge that the Earth is narrowing would affect my decision whether to visit you at Christmas. A positive confirmation of your hypothesis would undoubtedly tip the scales away from traveling, since I already have a horror of falling off.

Or do you mean "narrow" in some other sense? Honestly, sometimes I think we don't speak the same language. Perhaps you were using the word to connote "limited in outlook; without breadth of view or generosity; not liberal; prejudiced," as in the *Webster's New World Dictionary*. I can't believe you'd say that, when it was you who tried to discourage me from dating black guys in high school, not vice versa. In fact, up till now I've always thought you considered me a bit too open to new ideas and changing lifestyles.

So what's your gripe? A friend who just dropped by suggested you might wish I traveled in somewhat wider circles. Could that be it? Are you afraid I don't get around enough to insure my meeting up with Mr. Right? Well, put your minds at ease! I'll have you know I cruise the singles bars nearly every night looking for him. And just because most of my dates (at least by the harsh light of the morning after) are much too scuzzy to "bring home" to meet you, this doesn't mean I'm not doing everything I can to add to your collection of grandchildren — so keep those pacifiers handy!

Did I tell you I might go to jail? Probably not — it's so recent. Don't worry, though — I won't let it interfere with your birthdays!

My Belated Best Wishes to you and yours for a
Blessed Bennington Battle Day (see, I don't forget all
the important holidays).
>   With love,

>   Your Daughter
>   (Alias Bernice Balconey)
>   Colored Sheep

☞ BERNICE BALCONEY TO HER PARENTS (SENT)

>   October 12

Dear Mom and Dad:
    Did it never occur to you that living in a
community composed almost exclusively of retired
clergy couples might also be considered "narrow?"
Since we've been through this argument before, I
won't belabor my point except to say it hurts when
you show so little respect for my choices.
    My life is relatively calm these days. Aurelia is
still in New Hampshire. Once again I am lucklessly
looking for employment.
    Hope you are well.
>   Bernice

October 16

Dear Bernice,

Please be advised that you are skating on perilously thin ice with Judge Collins. In my professional opinion — which I am duty-bound to impart to you regardless of your devil-may-care attitude — there is considerable likelihood that he will increase your sentence on December 7 unless your behavior on that date is of an entirely different order from that to which he has become accustomed.

Please understand that I am not engaging in idle speculation when I state that Judge Collins is fast approaching the limits of his tolerance. In point of fact, I recently had a talk with him regarding your conduct at the October 12 hearing. Considering the probability that you will be cited for contempt if your demeanor does not take a radical turn for the better, it seems appropriate to recount the substance of that discussion in detail.

As I predicted in mid-September, the judge did not take kindly to your letter. In fact, only his already cramped calendar dissuaded him from sending the sheriff after you immediately. What he found particularly offensive about your letter was, in his words, its "criminally disingenuous" content. He was unable to decide whether to view you as a con-artist overplaying her role, or as — in his mind much the greater affront — a "spoiled brat college kid who doesn't know the meaning of respect." Either way he was predisposed to deal harshly with you.

Your attire in court — which I freely confessed to have been incomprehensible to me as well — was strike two against you. Bernice, I am utterly at a loss to understand why, at a hearing to prove indigency, you wore a slinky black dress, pearls, a mink stole, and brought two friends dressed respectively as chauffeur and lady-in-waiting. Although I have every confidence in the truthfulness of your representations to me regarding your actual financial state, Judge Collins can hardly be expected to deduce from your appearance that you are on the brink of starvation.

The last straw, the factor that did more to lose the case for you than any other, was a detail of your behavior that entirely escaped my notice. Judge Collins informs me that during my closing argument you winked at him several times, while puffing almost continuously on a cigarette holder containing a candy cigarette, and that you seductively bared one of your shoulders. Unfortunately, he still harbors a grudge against you for what he regards as — and I am inclined to agree — a gross impropriety.

It is possible to forestall going to jail by appealing Judge Collins' ruling to a higher court, as I have previously stated. Although I am dubious of success, that course of action would at least buy additional time in which to raise money for the fine. Your refusal to pursue this tactic is inexplicable to me. How am I to interpret your actions other than to conclude that you want to be incarcerated, both for non-payment of parking tickets and for contempt of court? If there is any other even somewhat implausible inter-pretation open to me, I would appreciate being advised of it.

In view of my long-standing relationship with you and your family, I am prepared to lend you the

money to pay the fine. And in order that you will not
have a debt hanging over your head, you may repay
me by helping to reorganize my law library. If this
arrangement is acceptable, please let me know right
away, and I will remove the December 7 court
appearance from Judge Collins' calendar. If not, you
should remember to bring a toothbrush to court.

At the risk of sounding somewhat more preachy
than is my custom, I urge you to show a little more
sense in this matter than your custom apparently
dictates. In fact, I will go even further, Bernice, and
state that I sometimes wonder whether you are not
burdened with inordinate quantities of unresolved
anger, and whether professional counseling might
not help you to deal with that. Please understand
that I say this not as a representative of your parents
but as someone who believes in your gifts and cares
that you use them.

Yours very truly,

Lily Barnstraw
Attorney-at-Law

☞ BERNICE BALCONEY TO LILY BARNSTRAW

October 19

My dear Lily (may I call you Lily?):

I'm surprised you didn't notice that I had Judge
Collins eating out of my hand. He stared at me
throughout your summation because he finds me

extremely attractive. I'm quite certain that he will amend his sentence to provide that I do my time helping him out around the court.

As for my attire, I regard it as a stroke of genius; not only was it absolutely appropriate under the circumstances, but it clinched our case for us. You see, after I wrote Judge Collins, but before the October 12 hearing, I did a lot of thinking about the popular truth that rich people get Justice but the poor do not. I now freely concede that it was a mistake to emphasize my poverty to Judge Collins, whose background leaves him totally incapable of identifying with anyone who was not born with a silver spoon in her mouth. When I realized that, I knew what I had to do — dress to the hilt, with all the trappings of richesse, so that he could not help but conclude that I had indeed fallen upon the proverbial hard times.

Have I dispelled all your doubts and anxieties? I certainly hope so, because I have always idolized and emulated you from afar. The last thing on earth I want to do is cause you pain.

Thank you for your kind offer of a loan. Fortunately, as I explained above, I will not be needing one. If you would like a nice dedication ode for your reorganized library, I am at your disposal.

With Unaffected Adoration,

Bernice Balconey
The Oldster's Odester

☞ BERNICE BALCONEY TO JUDGE COLLINS

October 19

My dear Reginald (may I call you Reggie?):

As I am sure you can imagine, my aristocratic breast heaved a sigh of relief the moment my little "secret" passed into the hands of so discerning and discreet a personage as yourself. Although I am, of course, aware that the weight of the Law is stacked against the privileged – especially those of noble birth like ourselves – I cannot but thank the Heavenly Broker that I need no longer engage in the pretense of belonging to the lower classes.

Judge Collins, I am a direct descendant of the great sausage magnate Luigi Baloney, who was himself of royal blood. That august gentleman, whose portrait still graces the Grand Ballroom of my stately but decaying ancestral mansion, Baloney Hall, was my great-great-great-grandfather. In addition, I am the widow of a dashing Resistance Fighter, Guiseppe Balconey, whose death during World War II left me permanently in mourning – and, I should add, in debt. As must now be eminently clear, my full name is Bernice Baloney Balconey.

The reason I did not "come clean" to you upon the occasion of my first appearance in court was that I did not at that time trust to your complete impartiality. When at last I discovered that your full name is Reginald Handywrap Collins, and it registered with me that Luigi Baloney and your great-great-grandfather had been childhood friends (in fact, I remember seeing an etching of the two playing leapfrog together), I felt deeply ashamed for ever having doubted your fairness.

48

Will you forgive me for this lapse of trust? Had my vision not been clouded by an intense headache, brought on by the tightness of the pencil through my head, I would have undoubtedly perceived in you a kindred spirit of the Blue-Blood — but alas, my condition blinded me to the dignity, propriety, and absolute elegance of your every gesture. A thousand pardons for this *faux pas*.

Now perfectly content to entrust my future to your hands, I will not resort to any of the tricks for which the poor are notorious, such as throwing myself upon the mercy of the court (which I understand is an immensely unflattering posture). Rather, with all the humility of my class, I shall simply state that I look forward to meeting you again under more congenial circumstances.

Thank you for your unfaltering magnanimity and rectitude.

Very graciously yours,

Bernice Balconey
Certified Aristocrat and
Blue Blood

☞ JOURNAL ENTRY BY BERNICE BALCONEY

October 19

Today I pondered the question "Am I a hack?" Visions of myself with a dull sickle, thrashing through a prairie afternoon, sunflowers and

milkweed crudely chopped, toppling at the ankles,
beaten down, sweat and milk co-mingling, souring in
the heat. I need a sharper blade, I said. And vowed to
reform my art.

☞ BERNICE BALCONEY TO AURELIA SIPES

October 23

Dear Aurelia:

Since you haven't responded yet to my letter
about Non-Monogamy (remember? It had to do with
SLEEPING AROUND), I can't help but conclude that
you're a little Jealous. Am I right, Aurelia?

Listen, there's no reason to be. So what if Rowena
Jaspers is independently wealthy, a fantastic lover,
and has all kinds of connections in the publishing
business! So what if she wants to whisk me off to
Paris for the weekend! After all, you've got your
worldly Jenny Fribbenz to teach you about poetry
and "real pain." What could be better for your literary
career than learning how to suffer?

In case it matters, Aurelia, my feelings for
Rowena have absolutely nothing to do with Love. In
fact, that's one of the beautiful things about Non-
Monogamy: it teaches you to take care of yourself by
rejecting Love as a four letter word. Self-love is okay,
as long as it doesn't spill over and mush up
relationships with other people — for, as everyone
knows, mushy relationships cause more pain each
year than Wars, Famine, and Pestilence have loosed

on humankind in all of recorded history.

No, Aurelia, Non-Monogamy sees Love for what it is: the desire to <u>own</u> another person. Heck, I don't want to own Rowena, I just want to kiss her all over her body.

I hope you come home soon so I can share this with you first-hand. You're still my best friend, and, as far as I can tell, there's nothing inherently possessive about that. If it turns out I'm wrong, if it turns out that the only truly unpossessive friendship is self-friendship, perhaps we can work something out around the fact of being roommates. If not, it's been swell, but it's time to move on to Higher Consciousness.

In the spirit of Non-Monogamy, I am free the third Thursday of November and would like to spend the night with you, dutch-treat, of course. R.S.V.P. by November 15.

> Signed,
> Everybody's Friend,
>
> Bernice Balconey

☞ ARTICLE AND INTERVIEW IN THE
NOVEMBER ISSUE OF *AMAZON:*
ATTENTION ALL FRUITS AND VEGGIES

On October 24, Bernice Balconey delivered an impromptu speech during a break in the concert by Circe and the Sirens at Sistermoon Feminist

Bookstore and Art Gallery. Ms. Balconey was wearing a wrinkled, moth-eaten, oversized cheerleader's costume with a huge gold "B" dangling across her chest by a few threads. She carried pom-poms, which she rattled sporadically. Since her speech aroused a great deal of interest and controversy, we have decided to publish the text in full. The following is an exact transcription of a tape made by Nora Bleeble:

Lovers, Ex-lovers, and Lovers-to-be:

The producers have generously granted me permission to address you during this lull in the concert. It seems there are some bugs in the sound system. I guess they're concerned that the poor critters will suffocate.

My friends, I ask you to consider whether the situation I am about to describe seems *just* to you. Forget for a moment that I will soon receive a large inheritance, which I plan to turn over to women's groups in Milwaukee. Think of me as a complete stranger rather than as the woman who will probably give you your next job.

Over the past six months, on approximately six occasions, I found under the windshield wiper of my car a yellow envelope marked "citation." Glancing over the printing on it, I realized that this citation had something to do with parking. On each occasion I observed the position of my car relative to the curb. Yes, indeed, it was parked — and what's more, I had done an exceptionally fine job of it.

Now, a "citation" in its most customary usage is an honorable mention for bravery or meritorious achievement, right? If you had been me, would you have concluded that the police wanted to punish you for something? I don't think so. I think you would have concluded, as I did, that you were being commended for a job well done.

The envelope also said something about five dollars. When I saw that I said to myself: "Far out! There's prize money too!" But when I looked inside the envelope it was empty. So, do you think I went down to the police station within ten days to demand my winnings? No! I'm a public-minded citizen. I let them keep their money.

From what I have just recounted, would you say I have done anything to deserve a jail sentence? Absolutely not! It is obvious that I am being framed by someone in a high place who wants me off the streets for a while. If I am to beat this bum rap, I will need help from all of you.

Someone suggested that I take up a collection to raise money to pay the fine. I am unwilling to do that. If I concede defeat by paying the fine, what is to stop the police from using this trick again in the future to harass one of us? The fact is, we cannot afford to allow injustices of this type to go unprotested.

I would like to invite all of you to attend my court hearing on December 7th. On that date, unless Judge Collins has a change of heart, I will be packed off to jail. I am asking that each of you show up, dressed either as a fruit or a vegetable, to show him someone cares. I'm sure he'll think twice about sending me up the river when he sees there are tens of women willing and able to continue my work on the outside.

The CCCWDWBBTGTJ (that's the Committee of Concerned Citizens Who Don't Want Bernice Balconey To Go To Jail) will be selling "Free Bernice Balconey" buttons at the door as you leave. The proceeds from the button sales will be used to make bumper stickers bearing the same message, whose profits will go into poster production, which in turn will subsidize the T-shirts, whose sale should give us enough capital to develop a whole new line of fall fashions. For a limited time only we are offering four buttons for the price of five. Get yours now while they last.

They're signalling me that the sound system is back in operation. It seems someone spilled a beer into the amplifier. Let's try and hold on to those beers, shall we, sisters?

In closing let me just say. . . What's that?. . . Oh. For the benefit of those in the back of the room, someone up front just asked me what I meant by "dressed either as a fruit or a vegetable." Well, you know, I mean like an apple or a zucchini or an onion, something like that. . . Why? Because naturally I plan to go to court dressed as a green pepper — and this is to be a show of solidarity, remember?

In conclusion, I would just like to say that I am grateful for having been given this opportunity to present my case to you. Special thanks to the woman who is lending us her produce truck to ride to court in. We'll meet here at 9:30 on the 7th.

And now, for your listening enjoyment, I give you Serious and the Serenes. . . Begging your pardon, that's Circe and the Sirens. Bring on the music!

* * * * *

One of the members of our staff collective, Nora Bleeble, interviewed Bernice Balconey on October 26 in her attic apartment. Ms. Balconey lives on the third floor of a dilapidated, corner storefront building. In the uninsulated half of the attic, she stores a hodgepodge of old typewriters, radios, televisions, bicycles, and miscellaneous "inventions" (as she calls them). The finished apartment contains two rooms and a small kitchen and bathroom. The interview took place in Bernice's "sitting room" (her words), which is furnished with a mattress, a spool table, stacks of books (which the two cats kept knocking over and Bernice kept patiently repiling), and two comfortable — if slightly gaudy — flower-print, overstuffed chairs.

Amazon: Bernice, there's been a lot of confusion about your speech at Sistermoon last Saturday. No one quite understands what you're trying to accomplish or what you'd like us to do. Would you mind explaining?

Bernice: I'd be glad to. In fact, being a person around whom confusion seems to congregate, I welcome the opportunity to make myself plain. Is that clear?

Amazon: Very.

Bernice: Now then... Where were we?

Amazon: You were about to explain your speech at Sistermoon.

Bernice: Oh, yes. A simple matter, really. I can't remember everything that was said, but I do recall there were problems with the sound system. Is that what you had in mind?

Amazon: No. It's your court case — the parking citations and all that.

Bernice: Oh, of course. Those lousy tickets.

Amazon: More specifically, you requested that everyone dress up either as a fruit or a vegetable and accompany you to court.

Bernice: Did I suggest that, really? Gosh. Well, it's a cute idea. I don't know that it would be particularly effective, but it does have a certain mouth-watering appeal.

Amazon: I guess the question still is: do you want support from the feminist community and, if so, what form should it take?

Bernice: Well, of course, support would be wonderful. Just terrific. As for the form it should take, heck, I don't want people putting themselves out. Just have them send whatever they can: liquor, drugs, spare change, canned goods, furniture, books, jigsaw puzzles, a stereo (I'd really love having a stereo), kitchen utensils, anything they don't need. Literally anything. I'm very resourceful. You should see the terrific refrigerator I made out of cardboard boxes. It gets a little soggy when I have to defrost, but it sure beats living out of a thermos bottle.

Amazon: That isn't exactly what I meant by support. My question was aimed at finding out whether you want us to do anything about your court case — you know, like attend the hearing on December 7th, demonstrate, or whatever.

Bernice: Definitely. Yes. That'd be a gas. I bet if we all dressed in black robes and powdered wigs, Judge Collins would mistake us for a group of visiting dignitaries from England. Then, in a desperate attempt to demonstrate the humaneness of the American judicial system toward its debtors, he might let me off scot-free. Yes, I like that plan a great deal. It has the additional merit of pointing up the feminist origins of Justice. You know, I have a theory that until comparatively recent times every judge in England was a woman, and that men only succeeded in entering the ranks through the transvestite deception of wearing long black dresses and wigs.

Amazon: Bernice, if you don't mind, I'd like to ask you a few questions about yourself, rather personal questions. Is it okay with you if we move briefly into that area?

Bernice: Certainly. My life is an open book.

Amazon: Good. What do you do to survive?

Bernice: Well, I smoke a lot of dope, and I subscribe to *Amazon.*

Amazon: No, what I had in mind was how do you support yourself?

Bernice: Oh, I get it. Income and all that. Well, there are a few sources I'm not at liberty to divulge, but I *can* say I've got a part-time job at Central Division.

Amazon: The mental hospital? What do you do?

Bernice: Well, mostly I impersonate a sane person and help out in the Occupational Therapy Department when they work with the women from the locked wards on Tuesdays and Thursdays. Assist the women in making pot-holders, that sort of thing.

Amazon: Is that a depressing job?

Bernice: Yes and no. Depressing in that most of the women don't belong there. Not depressing in that I probably do.

Amazon: You mean as a patient?

Bernice: Well, certainly not as a psychiatrist. I'm not that far gone.

Amazon: Bernice, I suppose you noticed that about half of the women present at your speech at Sistermoon gave you a standing ovation and the other half raised their eyebrows in disbelief. Your position in the women's community is. . . well, it's. . .

Bernice: Borderline? Tenuous?

Amazon: Something like that. People don't know what to think. Some women worry that you are mocking us.

Bernice: Then perhaps it would interest them to
know that until fairly recently I never even cracked
a smile. I was, in short, a humorless ideologue, totally
lacking in the vibrant wit and crackling good humor
for which feminists are justly renowned. That was
while I was working on my Ph.D. in Laundromat
Design and thought all the world's problems could be
solved through intelligent laundromat planning. If
my crude attempts to evoke laughter rubbed women
the wrong way on Saturday, maybe it's because I'm
still a novice when it comes to humor... There! My
secret is out, and I feel much better. Anything else
you'd like to know?

Amazon: Yes. What do you want us to do about your
court case?

Bernice: Actually, I don't feel I've hit on quite the
right formula for making my point, whatever that
turns out to be. If women are really interested to
know what's planned, they should call either me or
Judge Collins in a week or so — better yet, both of us,
if they want anything like a complete scenario.

Amazon: I want to thank you for talking to us...

Bernice: Thank you for listening. Talk is cheap,
listening a rare commodity these days.

Amazon: I feel that you've let us know you a little
better. Hopefully this interview will help straighten
out the confusion around who you are and what
you're up to.

Bernice: Good, then I'll definitely read it. I need to
know that stuff.

Amazon: Good luck in court.

Bernice: Thank you. The same to you.

October 31

Dear Bernice:

i can't tell u how happy i am to hear u're seeing
other people. i know u have a tendency to brood and
to cut yourself off and feel terribly lonely. It's great
that u're getting out in the world and finding out
how attractive u are to other women. i've thought for
a long time that u form unhealthy attachments, i
mean in the sense of wanting too much from just
one person. Now maybe u'll learn how to get little
bits of what u need from a lot of different people.
Maybe now u'll stop always being disappointed.

Oh, Bernice, i think u're wrong about Love. Love
doesn't have to be possessive or jealous, like u seem
to think. There are many different forms of it. For
example my poetry teacher, Jenny Fribbenz, (have i
mentioned her before?) told me yesterday that she
loves me, Bernice, and u know i think she does, in a
very quiet, gentle way, a *mature* sort of way that
makes me realize how young i really am and how
little i do know about anything at all. It's not that i
didn't/don't love u, Bernice, it's just that i'm not sure
u and i were/are very good for each other, i mean we
were both pretty mixed up about what we wanted to
do with our lives and therefore probably spent too
much time testing each other. In any case, Bernice, i
feel like i'm just starting to learn about love and i
think u should too before u go off being cynical about
it.

Well, that's enough preaching for one day,
Bernice. i'm happy for u. i'm sure Rowena is very
nice or u wouldn't hang out with her. i hope u have a

wonderful time and stay open to the possibility of
being happy. We both deserve the best.
            Love,

            Aurelia

☞ JOURNAL ENTRY BY BERNICE BALCONEY

                            November 7
Dear Diary:
    Do you know how it feels when your favorite
blue jeans suddenly self-destruct? It always happens
just at the point when you've got them perfectly
compliant, soft, responsive, faded, worn. Then they'll
rip across your fanny or a knee will go. The patch
you put on is useless to save them, but you try it
anyway because you can't bear the thought of starting
fresh. A week later, maybe less — more skin exposed.
It is possible to remake them, sure, by sewing patch
to patch, but that defeats the spareness that you're
after, the threadbareness that's so elegantly gentle
to the touch. Then you give up; they've passed, alas,
to imperfection. You cannot hold them to your use.
    Relationships are like that, too: just as they're
getting comfortable, a gaping hole appears. Then you
must choose whether to patch the imperfection or to
throw the thing away. On the one hand, patching is
work, simplicity is lost, love will never be the same.
But on the other, newness scratches, perfection
doesn't last, tearing inevitably happens.

Why do I say all this? I guess I'm upset that Aurelia has started referring to our relationship in the past tense and keeps mentioning that woman, Jenny Fribbenz. For my own sanity's sake I'm trying to remember all the hassles we had living together – in particular, the petty crimes she used to accuse me of (money jumped out of my pockets into other people's wallets; I did not pay bills, only attention – and some have questioned even that; I brought strange people home and then ignored them; I hid used kleenex in the cracks of chairs; I disparaged legitimate human needs, substituting the word "piracy" for "privacy" in conversation; I was inappropriately serious at times; I was rarely serious when the situation called for it; I opened other people's mail and answered it; I gave Aurelia's school chums the wrong address when we invited them for dinner; I embarrassed her at Department teas by showing up dressed as a bookworm or an ivory tower; I staged egg-hunts for kittens and forgot about the eggs they didn't find; and... oh, yes... I rarely talked about emotions (being of the school that says it's hard enough just feeling them).

Dear diary, I'm starting to think there's a chance Aurelia may not move back to Milwaukee. Can you imagine that? No more breakfasts in the bathtub, no more day-long dramatizations of Russian novels, no more egg-coloring bees!

I can hardly believe it. I knew when she left that we had problems, but I figured she'd miss my amusement-park ways. What I didn't reckon on, what I foolishly failed to consider, was that she might find someone else more congenial than living in a three-ring circus/freak show/cabaret. It's really quite a blow.

Dear diary, I have been through this before. It wouldn't be so painful — in fact, it might be funny — if I didn't in my lonesome heart believe that Aurelia Sipes is the most accepting and supportive lover I've ever had. The day she went away I could not laugh — shrilly, cynically, or otherwise — when she said, "No matter what happens to us, I will always be your friend!" (How many times have I heard those words from barely-remembered Great Enduring Loves of Years Gone By?) All I could do was suck in my pride and wait. Now I feel her slipping away, and there's apparently nothing I can do to hold her to me.

Oh well. Perhaps I won't even bother to tell her I made up most of that stuff about Rowena Jaspers. And why should I correct her if she thinks I'd never really pawn her things? (In truth, I didn't mean to.) Won't she be surprised to come home at Christmas to an empty apartment? Won't she be shocked to find me as alone as ever?

One thing is certain: I won't beg her for another chance. Bernice Balconey has her pride. I know when I'm not wanted. Aurelia had her chance and blew it.

Her loss.

                                    Bernice

☞ BERNICE BALCONEY TO AURELIA SIPES

                                    November 11

Dearest Aurelia:

Among other miscellany in the box of Mementos

(that's how I had marked the box: Mementos) that I recently found in the closet was a joint of unknown origins, which I just smoked, mostly as an experiment to see if it was any good, which it was, so I smoked all of it right away. And here I am. And there you are. So what's to be done with us?

You may, if you wish — not that I could stop you — regard this letter as a temporary set-back in my escalating struggle to prove myself worthy of the title Non-Monogamist (I'm scheduled to "fly up" any day now). Whatever you do, promise you'll never show this to anyone, okay? Untold horrors will befall me if word gets out that I actually wrote a Love Letter this close to initiation. And this is a love letter, you know?

Oh, Aurelia, do you also know what dope this is? It's the same stuff we smoked during the delectable bathtub dinner I prepared the night before you went away. How you could have left me after that dinner, that night, I will never understand. Why did you?

I wonder if you remember as clearly as I do the particulars of that scene: bayberry candlelight, peach blossom bubblebath, daisies in our hair, soyburgers and french fries on our plates, Ariel falling (hurling herself) into the bathtub, and you trying to teach her the doggie-paddle. Would it have helped if I'd cooked something more elaborate? At the time you said it was good, but I've often wondered whether soyafish and chips wouldn't have made the difference for you between leaving and staying. Please let me know what you think about this.

But won't you change your mind? I beg you, Aurelia, come home now. There's a cold, harsh world out there, and no one understands me. I'll never say a dispassionate word — just cook your meals, emote, clean house, do laundry, rub your back, change your typewriter ribbon, manage your money, and personally escort your school chums to our house for dinner. I'll turn over a new leaf, that's what I'll do. I'll take each kleenex down to the garbage the minute I'm through with it, laugh whenever Emily Post tells me to, bring strange people home and not ignore them, open other people's mail and not respond to it, and dress appropriately for your Department teas — even if this means renting a cap and gown.

Don't you understand that I'm lousy at taking care of myself? Doesn't it matter at all that Judge Collins is about to throw me in jail? Oh, Aurelia, none of this would have happened if you'd been around to cool me down. You know as well as I do that I'm not cut out to be a political prisoner. Won't you come home and rescue me? I'm at the end of my rope. I may even go straight!

Help!

Your Lonesome Co-conspirator,

Bernice

P.S. Don't worry. I won't implicate you in the crime, even if they try to torture the information out of me!

☞ WISCONSIN ARTS CONCLAVE
TO BERNICE BALCONEY

Madison, WI
November 17

Dear Ms. Balconey:

The Wisconsin Arts Conclave regrets to inform you that your proposed project, an Environment entitled "What Lesbians Do, has been found unsuitable for funding at this time. In the opinion of the Visual Arts Committee, your idea might be viewed as appealing solely to the prurient interests of the art public.

The Committee suggests the following changes: choose a more universal subject matter.

Should you bring your project into conformity with these suggestions, you are cordially invited to resubmit your proposal by the next deadline, which is: December 1.

Thank you for your interest.

Very truly yours,

Seymour Blodgett
Executive Director
Wisconsin Arts Conclave

☞ "PASTOR TAD" TO THE WISCONSIN ARTS
CONCLAVE (by Bernice Balconey)

November 20

Dear Wisconsin Arts Conclave:

One of my parishioners, Ms. Bernice Balconey,
recently received a letter from you denying her grant
request on the grounds that it "might be viewed as
appealing solely to the prurient interests of the art
public." I am writing in strident protest against your
decision.

Although I prefer to think of myself as other-
worldly rather than worldly, my profession puts me
in contact with more deviants each day than the
average person can hope to meet in a lifetime. By
virture of this contact, I think I qualify as an expert
on homosexuality. As such, I feel conscience-bound
to comment on your action relative to Bernice
Balconey's grant application.

First, I am shocked that you immediately
assumed Ms. Balconey's piece would be indecent or
immoral. Are you so full of lust and other sinful
cravings as to be unaware that not everyone shares
your depravity? I urge you to examine your hearts
and to root out the evil that led you so quickly to judge
and to condemn. Did not Our Heavenly Hero once
say: "Before you go fishing around for toothpicks in
your neighbor's eye, you'd better take the telephone
pole out of your own eye"? (from *The Swinger's Bible*,
page 816)

Second, my encounters with homosexuals have
taught me that what they "do" is as rich and varied
as life itself. Even assuming, for the sake of argument,
that Ms. Balconey intends to portray what lesbians

"do" in the <u>sexual</u> arena, I would not be surprised if
she showed them on their knees praying to Our
Merciful Masochist for strength to resist temptation.

I have known Ms. Balooney for many years, and
believe her to be a sincere individual as well as a
talented artist. It would be tragic indeed if she did
not have the chance to share her unique gifts with
the world because the Wisconsin Arts Conclave
jumped to erroneous conclusions regarding the
content of her work. I am sure I speak for many of
my members in urging you to reconsider your
decision.

Very truly yours,

"Pastor Tad"
Sodom Lutheran Church

☞ HER MOTHER TO BERNICE BALCONEY

Long Island
November 27

Dear Bernice:

We know you received the telegrams we sent,
because I checked with the Western Union. Well,
obviously it is too late to expect a visit from you at
Thanksgiving, but won't you please at least let us
know whether you can come home at Christmas?
Your Father and I would love to see you, and we know
you must be lonely without our Family being in
Milwaukee anymore. There's no reason to suffer in

silence, Bernice. If money is a problem, we might be able to help out a little. Please let us know how much you would need — within reason, of course (don't forget we are retired now, and money doesn't grow on trees).

And speaking of money, we really can't afford to send you telegrams and then have you just ignore them. Your Father said yesterday he wishes you would learn a little respect for other people's pocket books, especially when those other people supported you for many years and even sent you to college. It's not our fault you didn't like it there, he says. Well, 'nuf said, I hope.

We received a lovely note from Mrs. Gunderson last week. She mentioned that she is still not sure what you look like. Next Sunday why don't you introduce yourself to her? We mailed your address to the church, just in case the evangelism committee happens to be in your neighborhood and wants to stop in for a chat. (Please don't disgrace us, Bernice. We do worry about you and pray all the time that you will return to the fold, where you belong.)

Your Father just came in so I'll have to say good-by. He has a splitting headache, which always happens after he makes sick calls at the hospital. Strangers still take advantage of him when they see his clerical collar. I guess they think he should make himself available to any Tom, Dick, or Harry in the street! Oh well, nobody ever said being a shepherd — even just two days a week — would be easy.

Write soon.

     With love,

     Your "Mom"

☞ HER FATHER TO BERNICE BALCONEY

Long Island
November 30

Bernice:

Yesterday I telephoned Lily Barnstraw concerning my Will. When I inquired as to whether she had seen you lately, she admitted finally that she has been in regular contact with you for several months. She would tell me no more than that, but I did not like the sound of it. Bernice, I suspect that you are in some kind of trouble. I know it angers you when I ask questions about your life, but bear in mind that I have friends in Milwaukee, and that your behavior affects the whole family. If you are involved in some activity that threatens to destroy my credibility with former parishioners, I demand to be informed of it.

Your mother is taking this particularly hard. If the effect of your antics on me is of no concern to you, please remember that her health is no longer what it used to be.

Dad

☞ PRESS RELEASE: BALCONEY ELECTS JAIL
   (by Bernice Balconey)

December 3

Milwaukee, WI (Balconey Wire Service) — Bernice Balconey, noted inventor and entrepreneur, announced today that she is dropping her effort to obtain a pardon for non-payment of parking tickets.

Speaking to a small gathering of winos in Pere Marquette Park early this morning, Ms. Balconey stated unequivocally that she has had a "change of heart" and is now prepared to "go quietly" to prison. Sentenced on October 12 by Municipal Court Judge Reginald Collins, Balconey has until December 7 to come up with $120 or be sent to jail for six days.

"Sure, I could get the money," Balconey told the admiring crowd. "But that's not the point. The point is, I've done something naughty and I deserve to be punished."

Ms. Balconey further stated that she regards as "deplorable" the efforts made during the last century to abolish debtor's prison. "Fortunately, those misguided liberals succeeded only in changing the vocabulary, not the reality, of incarceration for non-payment of debts," she averred. "We would be in sorry shape indeed if poor people thought they could get away with poverty."

The soft-spoken Balconey elaborated by saying, "I'm going to jail to demonstrate my support for the concept of debtor's prison. This business of poor people using their indigency as an excuse for not having any money has got to stop. I hope my going through with this jail sentence will teach them a valuable lesson."

Asked by a spectator why she failed to pay her own parking tickets, Balconey replied modestly, "My horse ate them."

Despite the cold, regarded by some as the harbinger of an early winter, Ms. Balconey was cheered enthusiastically by the crowd of shivering winos at the conclusion of her remarks. Many expressed interest in joining her protest.

Judge Collins was unavailable for comment.

December 6
Jail Eve
3 a.m.

Dear Diary:

I'm totally broke, jail beckons like a carnival —
garish and unreal at this hour of night — and I
wonder what the hell I'm doing. Tomorrow I'll be a
prisoner in a dingy cell at the County Jail. For what
crime? No crime of passion, that much is clear. For
having a big mouth? Well, now we're getting closer.
For being stubborn? Yes, I suspect that's it: Bernice
Balconey is going to jail because she can't get it into
her kinky head that Reginald H. Collins has
power.Without the appurtenances of his office,
without the bailiff and clerk and city attorney,
without the weight of the Law behind him, Judge
Collins is a twirp. Lily Barnstraw, on the other hand,
has integrity and magnetism, she stands for
something, she cares about Justice — but whom must
she appeal to, whom must she flatter and cajole, on
whose whim does her success or failure rest? It rests
on him — the twirp (I hope he's flattened by it).

Why don't I just grit my teeth, swallow my pride,
and pay him off? That would at least save Lily the
embarrassment (and possible anxiety) of seeing one
of her clients carted off to jail. But I don't have any

money! Lily would give me the money if I let her, but I just can't do it.

Something happens to me when I am faced with blatant injustice. Or perhaps the problem is that I live in a state of perpetual temporary insanity. Whatever the cause, I lack the ability to play it safe, to do what is expected, to subject myself to the authority of bullies. Instead, I stand at a short distance away and stick out my tongue, I clown and taunt and jeer; then, when they come after me, I scurry under the sofa. Well, this time they caught me, and now I must decide whether to kiss their feet and hope they go away, or to taunt them at even closer range, whatever the cost to my safety.

I realize I may be making a mistake, but the truth is, I don't even want to turn back. For some reason — and I hope it isn't self-destructive — it seems almost appropriate to hurl myself into the mouth of the mechanical monster. I want to find out how rapacious it is, and how resourceful I am. Can't I charm and disarm it with a joke? Won't Judge Collins ever crack a smile? Doesn't the patriarchy have a sense of humor? One good belly laugh would disgorge an awful lot of the people it has swallowed. I'll have to bring a feather or a tickler and see what I can do. After all, the monster itself is only made of people glued together — by fear more than anything else. I believe in the explosive power of laughter. Soon I will find out whether humor really is the "release" I always count on it to be. Soon I will find out which is stronger: Judge Collins and his Laws, or the power of my jokes to make the system fly apart, or at least choke and spit me out.

Meanwhile, I'll console myself with making a

political statement, however futile. Milwaukee's night parking regulations, though minor in comparison with other abuses, are symptomatic of a larger problem, namely that our system of justice discriminates against poor people. My crime was not an offense against the orderly movement of traffic. My crime was that I didn't purchase a night parking permit or rent a garage, for the simple reason that I didn't have the money. For the same reason, I didn't pay the tickets, which meant that warrants were issued and bigger fines slapped on, until finally I'm on the brink of being sent to jail. Judge Collins apparently thinks there is something maliciously anti-social about my not having money. He doesn't understand that if it were up to me I'd get paid for my art and buy one of those damned permits just to keep the police off my back. Although I have no illusions about making Judge Collins see that what he's doing amounts to the reinstitution of Debtor's Prison, I can't give up trying, no matter how scared I am of going to jail.

I'll simply have to face the music. Yesterday I called the jail to find out whether they would let me write letters. They said yes, as many as I want. I may be doing that a lot, to keep my head together. Just writing this is helping.

I only wish I knew how to explain myself to Lily. I wish I knew how to thank her for wearing her soul on her sleeve, and for doing battle. I wish she'd let me make her a costume for tomorrow.

What will I do in court? I've no idea. It depends, I suppose, on how I'm feeling when I wake up on Monday, subject to change at the last moment. Let's hope I'm in a fairly mellow mood, and that I don't

provoke Judge Collins into throwing the book at
me — volumes of statutes are lethal weapons, and I
am not particularly quick on my feet in a cow
costume.

Wish me luck — I know I'll need it.
                    B.

☞ BERNICE BALCONEY TO AURELIA SIPES

County Jail
December 7-8

Aurelia:

Here is a very grungy Bernice Balconey shouting
faintly at you from the dungeon within that vast
fortress euphemistically known as the Safety
Building. Can you hear me? Are my pencil scratchings
too feeble, the toilet paper too grainy for you to
distinguish my heart-rending cries of agony, woe
and despair over my poor, wretched, wasted life, now
in shambles at my feet?

Despite the seeming finality of this place, a
distant hope glimmers. There's talk in here of an
uprising on the Outside — a tidal wave of popular
furor swelling, building, crescendo-ing, about to crash
over this castle-made-of-sand, smash these retaining
walls, snap these bars like reeds, swirl us, hurl us to
the very portals of justice, there to uproot our
accusers, cleanse them in the bath of the people's ire,
baptize them in the name of all that is fluid and
moving.

We political prisoners know that the people will not long tolerate a system in which Law and Order are allowed to trifle with the free, unfettered flourishing of Beauty and the Arts. We look with greedy anticipation to that glorious day when the people rise up and put their foot down, cry out with one voice: "You may not jail our creative spirits when they forget to pay their parking tickets! Art and artists are more important to us than filling the public coffers or keeping taxes down. Death to Boredom! Long live Creativity! Down with Inhibition! Up with Imagination!"

(Meanwhile, Reality comes crashing back — in the form of a guard who orders me to clean up the shambles at my feet. Oh, how I long for a day when my shambles and I are left to our own devices, to fester in peace according to our own internal rhymes.)

No doubt you are wondering what happened in court. Well, Aurelia, to assuage your hunger for details, I will attempt with this tiny stub of a pencil on this hard, hard concrete floor to set down my day exactly as it passed — fighting with my last ounce of strength to keep from passing out due to starvation, sleeplessness, and other unspeakable atrocities. So you just settle back in that comfy chair in front of your toasty fireplace, eat popcorn, sip sherry, and doze off whenever the sandperson wafts you away into your cozy dreamland — so many zillions of light-years from the cruel, hard, pitiless world where your faithful friend Bernice is about to faint from deprivation.

LATER: Whew! All that talk about unspeakable atrocities wore me out. I've just had a pleasant catnap, though, and am feeling greatly refreshed. Here is my story. Please treat it with the patience and sympathy I've seen you devote to aging pets and relatives.

It started last night at Choir Practice (no, this is not a flashback — we've gotten a women's chorus together. It only seems like a flashback because everyone acts the way they did in their church choirs and high school glee clubs. Actually, in all truthfulness, everyone acts worse than they did in high school. Especially the second altos, who now sing tenor much of the time — and let us remember that the altos were always the rowdiest section of any girls' choir. I don't know what it is about women singing in the lower ranges, but it seems to fill us with a sense of our own power, and, more immediately, our own physical strength. So we second altos guzzle beer, belch, put our feet up on the tops of chairs, and talk about getting a second alto motorcycle gang together. Get the picture? We act the way we always wanted to act at church choir practices but couldn't because our fathers were the pastors, or the presidents of the congregation, or trustees — and besides, we still had fantasies of growing up to be "normal," in the snuggle-bunny sense of that word.) Anyway, Nora Bleeble, who went to the same church and parochial school I did and sang in many of the same choirs, suggested to our Indomitable Directress that we do a medley of prison songs as a kind of salute to me on my last night of freedom. But to get the full flavor of what transpired you will need to know more about the group dynamic.

From the start, the question of who would lead

our merry group in song was problematical. Since we are a women's choir, we are naturally opposed to any kind of hierarchical structure, any on-going leadership. We experimented for a while with everyone directing herself but found it virtually impossible to swing both arms and read music at the same time — and besides, we kept poking our faces with our batons.

Clearly one director would be much more efficient. But who? We decided that we all would benefit from learning how to conduct a choir, and, consequently, settled upon the idea of a rotating directressship.

Now, on the night in question, the Directress was none other than yours truly, dressed appropriately in tails and cummerbund. (Parenthetically, I caught a bit of a sniffle because, as you know, tails do not cover all that much territory, even when you have several, as I did, from various animal costumes found lying about the house; and my cummerbund, while it protected the sensitive midriff section, left the rest of my body exposed.) Someone suggested that I roll myself up in a blanket, but when I pointed out to the group that we will never be invited to sing in the great concert halls and opera houses of Europe unless we maintain rigorous professional standards, everyone came around to my position — quite literally, in fact: we found a little stool for me to stand on, the choir huddled up close to keep me warm, I swung my baton as high and wide as I could reach, and people craned their necks to follow my directions. The tonal quality quickly degenerated from its normal level — the sopranos uncertain and faltering, the altos rather like a foghorn – to a steady moan of agony as their necks cramped or the women toppled over backwards.

We experimented with various methods of keeping the group together, such as buckling the motorcyclists' belts together around the outside of the huddle, but when we realized that one casualty would pull the whole group down on top of her, we decided instead to have everyone on the perimeter of the circle wear a motorcycle helmet and link arms. Unfortunately, our helmeted sisters could no longer hear to sing, and we had finally to ask them just to mouth the words. That put a serious strain on the rest of the group's enthusiasm as well as on their voices, and I began to wonder in earnest whether rigorous professional standards aren't a lot of hype perpetrated on the American people by the manufacturers of formal wear.

(As another aside: just as I was writing the above, a matron came by with a bologna sandwich for me. Well, being a firm believer that everything happens for a reason, I wondered, "What am I to learn from this? Is the bologna sandwich some kind of cosmic commentary on what I've been saying? Is someone playing a prank with my maiden name? Or am I really going to starve to death, since I can't stand bologna?" You'll be pleased to hear I did what every red-blooded American would have done under the circumstances. I screamed: "Go ahead, torture me! You'll never get me to talk! I'd sooner starve than tell you that Aurelia Sipes was my accomplice for every one of those parking tickets!")

Where was I? Oh, yes. We began to question whether rigorous professional standards aren't some kind of capitalistic and patriarchal ploy to keep us cool and distant from one another. We consciousness-raised around that and decided we'd rather look and sound terrible than give up having a good time. Those of us who are cursed by a weakness for excellence, perfection, or getting things done realized that these qualities can't be forced but will just naturally evolve out of our good feelings for each other. And the women who are tone-deaf resolved to get hearing aids. Isn't it amazing what the collective process can accomplish in a few short hours?

So, in place of rigorous professional standards we adopted lax amateurish fantasies. In general, women would be permitted to dress and behave as they liked, but some effort would be made to respect the Directress' peculiar foibles. This meant that I, as Directress-for-a-Day, had the perfect right to try to foist my "bizarre musical tastes" — as someone else expressed it — on the rest of the group, but no one could be coerced to come along with me.

Accordingly, I batoned us to order and resumed my private struggle to bring a little consonance to our orgy of noise. Cursed by an eye for music, I became increasingly agitated as I perceived that the sounds emanating from women's mouths bore little resemblance to the shape, color, and texture of sounds that have traditionally been labelled "on key." This posed a bit of a dilemma: should I point out to the group that according to conventional musical standards we probably sounded icky — which might make the choir angry or defensive — or should I ignore my misgivings and risk being called to task by other choir members who might think it my duty as Directress to bring these annoying details to everyone's attention.

Thank the Goddess for Nora Bleeble, who chose that very moment to suggest a medley of prison songs in my honor. Perhaps she noticed my discomfort and mercifully determined to bail me out. On the other hand, now that I think on it, she might have instigated that riot of cacophony to test my reactions. But whatever her motive, I was overjoyed to be let off the hook — and since good ol' Nora seemed eager to take charge, I gratefully sank into an easy chair, lifted my feet onto the end table, and breathed a mighty sigh of relief.

Can you guess what happened next? As if on signal, the room started filling up with women. I searched the end table for a secret button I might inadvertently have pressed, but found nothing. Before I could lift a questioning eyebrow to Nora, the assembly broke into a resounding chorus of "I've been working on a chain-gang, all the live-long day," followed by "Did she ever return, no she never returned" and excerpts from "Jailhouse Rock." It was a surprise party for me. Can you believe it? And here all day I'd been thinking I'd just have to tell Judge Collins I don't want to go to jail, because I haven't been at all in the right mood for prison lately. Well, let me tell you, with all those wonderful women singing those inspirational songs and handing me beer after beer, it didn't take long to get into the spirit of the occasion.

Now, Aurelia, I know how impatient you sometimes get with me for being — how shall I say — "Round-about." Forgive me if I'm wrong, but I can almost hear you saying: "Alright, already! Get on with it. What happened in court?" Well, if you're going to be that all-fired insensitive, skip to the next page of this letter. I urge you to consider, however, that you're playing into their hands. They would like nothing more than for you to believe that their systems and institutions are what's really important, not some silly merry-making by the people who care more about you than anyone else does in the whole wide world.

Now do you understand where I'm coming from, Aurelia? You'll never even get this letter; they'll burn it as subversive propaganda. They don't want the world to know they torture people with bologna sandwiches. Even as I write this they're out in the corridor jangling keys and slamming doors to distract me from my truth-inspired work. If I can persist against such seemingly insurmountable obstacles, cannot you? Won't you have a little tolerance for the demented ravings of a doomed soul?

LATER (earlier?): Real sleep must not be in my cards tonight. I did doze off for a bit – long enough to have a nightmare of Judge Collins saying to me, "Young lady, we have our ways of teaching non-conformists to respect the Law." That's pretty much what he said in court, but this time the emphasis on "WE HAVE OUR WAYS" made it sound a great deal more like a threat I should take seriously. And you know, despite my joking around I've understood all along that Judge Collins' "WE" doesn't include me. Perhaps the dream was a karmic reversal of my earlier speculations about "They" and "Them." On the other hand, isn't it also possible that Judge Collins doesn't like me?

MY DAY, CONTINUED: Now, of course, no send-off party is complete without a ritual. Clearly the time had come to give ourselves over to the spiritual side of our natures. In pursuit of this aim we piled into automobiles and hurried home to change costumes. By about 2 a.m. we were ready to ritual, and ritual we did.

Rather than concentrate our energies directly on something so mundane as court or jail, we determined to go back in time and seek the spiritual guidance of our paganistic foremothers. Floating down the Milwaukee River on a barge as Cleopatra and her entourage was passed over in favor of conducting a festival in honor of Aphrodite on the shores of Lake Michigan.

Unfortunately, our unanimity broke down over the question of which school of lyric poets would summon Aphrodite to our aid. I, for one, never having been satisfied that Sappho's alleged rival, Gorgo — whose work did not survive — was necessarily the lesser poet, held out for a diversity of viewpoints. In consequence of our stalemate it was decided that we would conduct a jingle bee to settle the matter. This good-natured competition we quickly dubbed the First Annual Aphrodite Aphroditty Bee.

In the interests of time, the contest rules as finally adopted by the rules committee provided that each side choose one woman to act as its spokesperson. The two spokespersons would trade jingles back and forth until one of the sides collapsed from exhaustion. All of the jingles had to be rendered within a ten-second time limit and attempt to lure Aphrodite to Milwaukee. If the three-judge panel determined that a proferred jingle did not conform to these standards, it would stop the match and award the prize to the other team.

My side, the Gorgettes, elected me to be our spokesperson as soon as I reminded them that I would probably have to go to jail that afternoon. The representative of the Sapphettes was Rowena Jasper. Everyone gave her the edge because she is a prolific songwriter. What they failed to reckon on was that I, as the champion rhymer of Grade Two, also had a reputation to uphold.

The Jingle Bee went on for longer than expected. I won't bore you with an exact transcription, but here are a few examples of our work (I can't remember who said what):

Aphrodite, if you'll come to Milwaukee
We promise not to be too gawky.

The Gorgettes invite you to visit.
That's not so terrible, is it?

Aphrodite, if you come down to Lake Michigan
We promise we won't ever fish again.

Two bits, four bits, six bits, a dollar,
If you come down here we won't have to holler.

Lake Michigan is one big polluted mess.
That's why it needs an Aphrodite caress.

Aphrodite, come down from the sky.
We'll give you a soyaburger on rye.

Aphrodite! Milwaukee women are cool!
Won't you please join us for a dip in the pool?

Get the picture? Anyway, this had been going on for nearly twenty minutes when someone noticed a robed figure coming straight at us down the side of the hill.

We screamed with delight. "It worked! It worked! She's here!" we shouted. And some of us sang; some of us clapped our hands; some of us squealed; some of us took off our clothes; and some of us — probably not too many — asked ourselves, in the privacy of our own sleeves, "I wonder which jingle caught her fancy. Doubtless one of mine. I'll have to inquire."

At this, the descending figure tripped over her own hem and took a nasty tumble. We rushed to her aid — but when we got there, our Aphrodite had been transformed into Elise Hackbarth, wearing a faded, paisly contour sheet and red galoshes. We were — need I say it? — disappointed.

Elise, it turns out, got left behind in our paganistic scramble to the lake and had to walk more than two miles to catch up. Given her discomfort, and our feelings of guilt, we were hardly in a position to complain.

So we did the next best thing. We took her out for breakfast.

And speaking of breakfast, it's that time already! I hope you enjoyed this letter.

Having a wonderful time — wish you were here. Write soon.

With love,

Bernice

P.S. Just realized I didn't tell you what happened in court. Sorry — I'll try again in another letter. Bear with me, okay? It's hard enough just holding it together.

P.P.S. Remind me, next time, to bring ear plugs and valium. I'm not cut out for this.

☞ BERNICE BALCONEY TO LILY BARNSTRAW
(UNSENT)

County Jail
December 8

Lily:

I doubt that I will send you this, but there's something I have to get off my chest. It's about this ANGER business. Remember your last letter when you suggested that perhaps I should DEAL WITH mine?

Well, you were wrong. I took a peek at it. What a horrible mistake! No one could love that warty, disgusting, sadistic, cowardly freak. No one. Least of all me.

I'm sorry I listened to you. For though I denied the validity of what you said, I did not forget it. Face my anger? No, Lily. I would sooner be stuck for the rest of my life telling the same stale joke than go out in a burst of uncontrollable rage.

These are my choices: make people laugh, or bludgeon them with a fury they neither created nor can understand. I don't think that in my case there's any in-between. I can hardly afford to go to the other extreme and find out, since it seems quite likely that I wouldn't come back.

This is a horrid place: four people crammed in a

tiny cell with a filthy toilet, grungy walls, bad lighting, bruises to nurse, and surly, spiteful treatment from the guards. It is demeaning and dehumanizing and makes us much less than a sum of angers. It is no wonder we go out and kill again.

Bernice is just barely maintaining. She is remembering how if your father is never home and your mother is always sick, you can get the idea they don't care. Except they do care if you fidget in church or mess up in school, but that's no fun cuz you get punished! The fun part, the really fun thing is making the other children laugh. That is what she always likes to do, whatever the cost.

And there are some other matters too. Such as, which side are you on? The Fuckors or the fuckees? Do you stand for Appearances, Order, Conventions — or are you real? Which is it, Lily? She needs to know.

She says sometimes you are disarmingly candid. You leave yourself open in ways that are professionally risky. But maybe that is because you know their language too and can snap into it at any time. Isn't it possible you will go there and not come back? She needs to know.

Love,

Me

County Jail
December 8

Dear Lily:

I hope you aren't upset that I'm in jail. It's really
quite a lovely place. In fact, it's so much like a college
dormitory that I'm feeling right at home.

Another wonderful thing is that they never
censor the mail we send out. For example, if I wanted
to tell you – and please understand that this is all
purely hypothetical – that THEY TORTURE PEOPLE
WITH BOLOGNA SANDWICHES, all I'd have to do is
come right out and say it. Or if I hoped you'd
ORGANIZE A DEMONSTRATION against, oh, say,
some GIGANTIC RATS, I wouldn't need to hem and
haw.

But enough of this praise. What's happening in
your life? Have you eaten any good CAKE lately? And
speaking of that, my case wasn't exactly a piece of
one, was it? Gosh. I bet my FILE is about TWO INCHES
THICK and about EIGHT INCHES LONG by now.

I'm always amazed at how time FLIES when I'm
having a good time. Did I mention how excellent the
FOOD is in here? Those crazy stories about prison
food being RANCID and PUTRID and MAGGOTY and
INEDIBLE absolutely MAKE ME PUKE.

PARDON me if I seem to be getting carried away
with praise. It's just that I think the food is so good
here that it should be served to the GOVERNOR or
the PRESIDENT.

And the prison library is impressive, too. The
books aren't all ESCAPE literature, either. In fact,

I'm sure I'll learn enough here to climb up a few rungs on the LADDER to higher consciousness. THE DAY AFTER TOMORROW at 3 A.M. I plan to start reading INTERIOR COURTYARDs of the soul by that great Eastern mystic C.U. THEN.

Well, time to sign off. It's been great chatting with you. Tell all my friends I'll be recommending some fabulous new titles to put ON THE RACK at Sistermoon Feminist Bookstore, and that I'm not in HORRIBLE PAIN or anything. I hope none of them are being POISONED by bitterness at my plight. And I don't want them going around saying JUDGE COLLINS IS A PRICK for putting me here.

Love and kisses,

Bernice Balconey
Model Prisoner

☞ BERNICE BALCONEY TO JUDGE COLLINS

County Jail
December 9

Dear Judge Collins:

Let's let bygones be bygones, shall we? After all, Christmas is only two weeks away, and we wouldn't want Santa's radar picking up vindictive vibes between us. I'm sure the Napoleon costume you've asked for is much more important than pampering your paranoia toward me.

And speaking of me, I'm doing just fine, thank

you. At first, I was angry with you for slapping those three extra days onto my sentence for "contempt of court," but now that I've witnessed the conditions here at County Jail, "contempt" seems like a mild word, and three days are a drop in the bucket compared to the incredible waste I see around me.

One of the women in my cell was raped at the age of five by her father; when she was twelve he started selling her body to his friends. He's a "respected" member of the community. She's a prostitute — because she thought she couldn't be anything else, and because the man who finally "liberated" her from her father turned out to be a pimp. A few days ago he beat her till she was almost unconscious. She's charged with attempted murder for defending herself. He's out on the street.

And then there's Mary, who's shivering right now on her bunk. She's been a heroin addict since before she was born. She got nabbed trying to steal quarters from a soda machine.

Denise, my third cellmate, was forced by her boyfriend and his buddies to accompany them on a gas station stick-up. She's been charged as an accomplice and is fightin' mad about it — stalks and stomps and swears. She's definitely on the road to trouble.

Well Judge Collins, I guess I've learned my lesson. Here I thought I was a pretty terrible criminal — what with parking illegally so many times — but now that I've met these women I finally know what evil is.

Fortunately, I've decided to clean up my act. In fact, to keep myself from becoming part of the "filth" you warned me of in court, I'm appying for a job as a laundromat attendant rather than as a judge. Since you suggested on numerous occasions that I find employment, I'm counting on your wholehearted support in this effort. Accordingly, I have taken the liberty to write and enclose a letter of recommendation. All you need do is sign, seal,and drop it in the mail.

Thank you, Judge Collins, for giving me the opportunity to rub elbows with the "criminal element" for a few days. The experience has given me more insights into our system of Judgment than you will ever know.

Yours in Law and Order,

Bernice Balconey
Rehabilitated Scum

☞ LETTER OF RECOMMENDATION
by Bernice Balconey

December 9

To Whom It May Concern:

In my opinion, Bernice Balconey is uniquely qualified to work as a laundromat attendant. I have never known her to overload a washing machine, nor is she injudicious in her use of detergent.

But objective criteria, such as the above, do not scratch the surface of character, which as a "reference" I am duty-bound to illumine. If you are half as cautious as I when it comes to hiring, you will want to test the essence of Bernice Balconey before placing her in a position of trust. Fortunately, as her soul's familiar, I am singularly equipped to comment on both her secret self and her public personality.

The psychic connection between Bernice and myself is so strong that it almost feels as if we have known each other all our lives. Beyond that, our astrological charts are remarkably compatible, and each of us has experienced vague memories of prior-life association. So you see, when I presume to interpret Bernice for others, I am not engaging in mere speculation.

For your purposes, the relevant features of Bernice's character are doubtless the following: she is honest (if anything, to a fault); she is clean of mind and body, pure of spirit; she is deeply committed to the institution of laundering and will do everything within her power to see that your establishment flourishes; she is friendly, courteous, and attentive to details; and she knows how to count without using her fingers

But perhaps you are concerned about her aristocratic past. This question in particular may trouble you: will Bernice adjust graciously to her reduced circumstances, or will waiting on others prove abhorrent and intolerable to her? Being myself a man of wealth and family, I believe I have insights on this point that you as riff-raff could not possibly share.

In your circle it is commonly, and, I might add, erroneously assumed that aristocrats like myself and Bernice Balconey have nothing but contempt for the hoi polloi. Although I personally would sooner starve than engage in manual labor, a stereotype that puts all of my class in the same boat is manifestly unfair to those of my equals who are turned on by the fantasy of being poor. It happens that Bernice Balconey, like Marie Antoinette, belongs to this perfectly respectable group of peasant-pretenders. As a result, not only will she _not_ put on airs, but it seems extremely unlikely to me that she will make so much as a single disparaging remark against people who soil their clothes. If anything, she will bend over backwards to appear humble. In a democratic society it should not be necessary to remind anyone of the above, but where prejudice is rife, let it never be said that Reggie Collins stood idly by while others denigrated his peers.

In conclusion, I urge you to hire this charming and resourceful woman, who is almost like a daughter to me. Should you question my qualifications as a judge of character, please bear in mind that your side lost the last election. And the next time you appear in my courtroom, be sure to ask for a personalized demonstration of my powers of discrimination.

Non-coercively yours,

Reginald H. Collins
Influential Person and Member,
Laundromat Licensing Commission

County Jail
December 10?
4 a.m.

Aurelia:

What hour is it? What day? Next time I go to prison I will know to pace myself. I forgot I never sleep in strange places. And jail is a strange place, dear Aurelia. You can believe me on that one.

Twyla Two-lips, my neighbor, sings a cantata. Beautiful voice, carries me home to church music. Hooking my heart like she hooked a policeman. Only I won't turn her in.

There is something very odd. I have the shakes. Probably from lack of sleep, insufficient body heat, not enough internal combustion. Stoke me up somebody, I'm losing momentum.

Cold coffee. Ice cube cold, this coffee. Nothing warms me up. If only I knew how to be sentimental. That'd do for a few calories. Think of my kindergarten teacher. Sit on someone's lap and cuddle, huddle against the freeze.

Ponder something different, change the subject, forget where you are and how you feel. Literature. Now there's a topic. Always good for a heated debate.

What place for male literary influences? No place! Shed them, unwed them, wipe the slate clean, chlorinate, fluoridate, and vaccinate against them. Purge yourself and start over. What? Even if that were possible, what would we gain? Book-burners, are we? No better than they? Aren't we wise enough to learn from what is helpful and discard the destructive?

There! You see? Already I feel better.

Love,

Bernice

☞ BERNICE BALCONEY TO HER PARENTS
(UNSENT)

County Jail
December 10

Dear Mom and Dad:

This letter will not be fluff-without-substance,
merely. It will lack good taste as well.

I am in jail. Your prophecies for me have all
come true. Perhaps someone will write a Book of the
Bible on you.

Truly I have seen the arrow of my ways. If it
sticks in your heart (which grieves – quite properly –
for loss of reputation), be cheered by my inestimable
gain (this lesson learned: "Children, obey your
parents. Suffer, you little ones. Father knows best,
amen." I Galoshes 2:10).

I'm so ashamed of my behavior that I almost
mortified my flesh. Please forgive this disgraceful
lapse into Papism. It was only momentary, though.
With the help of the Complete Works of Martin
Luther – which naturally I smuggled into jail with
me – I was able to stand firm against temptation.

In your last letter, you pronounced that my

behavior affects the whole family. If you're speaking of the Balconey family, what's it to you? Surely you can't mean your family. I told you ages ago when I started going by the name of Bernice Balconey that all my blood affiliations with you were at an end, and that you should regard me as an orphan or charity-case. That was in fifth grade, remember? I decided to spare you the opprobrium attached to my application for batgirl with the New York Yankees. To my mind that was a terrifically responsible step for a fifth grader to take — and all you cared about was how the congregation would react when they found out I'd disinherited you.

But enough of this reminiscing! You'll be pleased to learn that a group of friends and I are starting a choir. Many of us sang with church choirs for years and miss all that magnificent religious music. We're even talking about doing Handel's Messiah! Are you impressed? You should be — especially when you hear that I'm the one everybody chose to rewrite the lyrics!

Well, got to run. I'll be in touch after my term is up. Don't bother to send any cakes with files in them —

I've got all the reading material I need.

> Signed,
> Your Obedient,
>
> Bernice Balconey
> Orphan and Charity-Case

December 10

Dear Mom and Dad:

It seems like all you ever care about is what the neighbors will think. Isn't there supposed to be more to our relationship than that?

I'm afraid a Christmas visit is out of the question; finances and job interviews preclude a family holiday this year. I'll be thinking of you, though.

Please give my love and Christmas cheer to the whole family, especially my nieces and nephews. Needless to say, my biggest regret in all this is not getting the chance to practice changing diapers, in preparation for the day I find a family of my own (exactly where should I look, again?)

Here's hoping yule have a merry Christmas tide —

Ho ho ho —
With love,

Bernice

County Jail
December 11

Dear Wisconsin Arts Conclave:

In the past few weeks you have undoubtedly
read so many tidy, prim, and good-natured grant
proposals that you will have little charity for a hand-
scrawled letter on toilet paper, such as you now hold
in your hands. My response to your squeamishness
is this: tough bananas, WAC! The only other writing
surface available to me here at the Milwaukee County
Jail is the Warden's behind, and I'm sure you don't
want HIM lying around unopened for three months
on some half-forgotten desk in your office.

Let's get down to brass tacks for a moment, shall
we? Perhaps you're saying to yourselves, "This letter
is more than a week late. We don't even have to
consider it." Well, put that thought right out of your
heads; in fact, pack it off to Honolulu so there's no
chance you'll choke on it later. For your own
protection, I think you should know that fifteen
extremely-talented but slightly-crazed female
offenders — in whose behalf I am writing this letter —
are eagerly anticipating your prompt and affirmative
response. Although naturally I am opposed to
violence and will do everything within my power to
keep them from acting rashly in the event that you
turn down their proposal, I can make no guarantees.
In consequence, I urge you to give this application
your careful consideration — as you go about quietly
fortifying your homes.

The aforementioned extremely-talented but

slightly-crazed women — for whom I am a mouthpiece only — have conceived a plan to publish their collected writings in book form. They have assured me that somehow or another, by hook or by crook (no pun intended), they will lay their hands on a printing press with which to print the volume on their own.

They are asking $10,000 to cover expenses of completing, gathering, and editing the material, and another $50,000 to publish 500 copies. If the printing costs are a bit steep it is because, as someone mentioned to me the other day, each book will contain a secret compartment for storing valuables. Isn't that a terrifically imaginative idea? Gosh, these women are sharp! I think there's a great future for them in business. Respectable citizens like ourselves should do everything we can to encourage them to get involved in legitimate enterprises like this one.

As for distribution, my clients assure me there will be no problem on that score. Several say they've already had lots of experience "dealing" things out, and between the bunch they appear to have "connections" in every major U.S. city. For my own part, I am genuinely impressed at how much innate business acumen these women display for relative beginners. If I didn't know better, I'd say some of them have really been around.

Since I have agreed to supervise this project, please make the check payable to me and mail it to my home address. I hope you will not hold the somewhat harsh tone of the first two paragraphs against me; at the time I was writing them, two of the women were reading over my shoulder, and I thought it wise to take a hard line. I'm not really one of them, you understand; I'm just passing through on my way to Truth and Beauty. That does not mean, however, that you should disregard what I said about the possible nasty things that could happen to you if a check for $60,000 is not promptly forthcoming.

Altruistically yours,

Bernice Balconey
Model Prisoner and
Matron of the Arts

☞ BERNICE BALCONEY TO THE GOVERNOR OF WISCONSIN

County Jail
December 12

Dear Governor:

This is not one of those "crack-pot" letters you get every day from prisoners begging for pardon or commutation of sentence or asserting their innocence. I have more important things to do than grovel for sympathy. Right now I am engaged in working out the details of a thorough-going crime reform bill, which I am sure you will find most appealing. It is not based on misguided notions of making the punishment fit the crime, or other pie-in-the-sky theories of retribution and rehabilitation. Rather, it is based on dollar and cents practicality. In my own humble opinion, this plan is so revolutionary that it might even put Wisconsin on the map — a result that you, as Governor, should applaud for its tourist potential alone.

My idea came to me while reflecting on the fact that a lot of "criminal types" — most notably policemen, soldiers, athletes, politicians, and businessmen — find "legitimate" outlets for their aggressions. This led me to question whether the solution to crime might not be to provide more such outlets. At first I considered a federal program that would, for example, send politicians to the public schools to teach "problem" kids how they might use their anti-social tendencies to great advantage in government careers. Although this plan would take care of the juveniles, I later realized that much more drastic measures would be needed to aid habitual offenders — whose lengthy prison records presently deter them from obtaining any of the above so-called "respectable" positions. Here, then, is what I came up with for people who are already "hooked" into a life of crime:

Why not make stealing the national sport? Oh sure, I know what you're going to say: it already is the national sport. Then I say, let's legalize it so we can regulate it.

The first step would be to require thieves and embezzlers to purchase a license for their activities. The license would spell out appropriate regulations, including the opening and closing dates of the "season" for that crime. The monies obtained by the state through license fees would be used to set up prizes for the "funniest crime," "the most ingenious crime," and so forth. Rather than allow the criminals to keep any loot or money stolen, the victims would present them with a suitable trophy, medal, or prize commemorating their success. The value of the prize would be in direct proportion to the value of the goods stolen.

The state could also license stores, businesses, or private homes as target zones for crime. These establishments would display their licenses in a prominent place to notify criminals that they are fair game. They would then match their wits against the criminals. If successful in foiling a crime, they would be awarded a trophy, medal, or other prize by the criminals. They would also be eligible for prize money from the state.

This plan has the virtue of making certain types of crime completely self-regulating. Although it may be necessary at the start to offer license-fee scholarships to poor people (or provide a mechanism whereby they can steal them), the plan should ultimately support itself as well. Within a year or so, criminals should be able to make a comfortable living from prize money, TV and movie rights, books, magazine interviews, commercial endorsements, consultant fees, and the like. Instead of being a drain on state revenues, many criminals would become tax-paying citizens.

Policemen, prison guards, and judges who were put out of work by this plan could either revert to being criminals or else put themselves at the service of target stores and businesses. Presumably the best crime foilers would also find their work lucrative as well as challenging. The money saved by the state under this plan could be used to hire sensitive and skilled personnel to deal with violent crimes.

Well, Guv, what do you think? Pretty sound idea,

no? Not only would it take the risk out of bribery, influence-peddling, and embezzlement in government, but it would also allow government officials to don their "criminal hats" in public. I've always thought it must be a drag for politicians to have to cover up their most cherished skills.

If you have any questions on my crime reform bill, feel free to pardon me, commute my sentence, or offer me a high-paying job. I am always willing to put my civic duties ahead of my own personal convenience.

Yours very dutifully,

Bernice Balconey
Convict with Convictions

☞ JOURNAL ENTRY by Bernice Balconey

County Jail
December 13

I went up on the roof, in my imagination, to survey Milwaukee. It was near dusk, and the reddish-golden cast of the sun — ricocheting in slow motion — missed no one. All the world stood mute as if for something special, a twinkling of truth, perhaps. For thirty seconds no lying or deception — only awe. Deferred cruelty, frozen time, suspended animation.

Still, being a jailee with already too much numbness on my hands, I was inclined to feeling sorry. In reverence for the moment I muffled my wailing with a sweater, till it emerged a small roar: "Woe is me."

Then who should appear but my Muse, disguised as a street-walker, recognizable only by her cavernous eyes.

"Melpomene!" I called, self-righteously. "How dare you sell yourself so cheap!"

"Cheap!" she sneered. "I hear $120 in parking tickets will buy you for nine days. That's about fifty cents an hour."

She had a point. I let the matter drop.

"You know, Melpomene," I said contritely after a long silence, "sometimes people make mistakes, get in over their heads, bite off more than they can chew. Have you no compassion?"

"I have. When it's appropriate."

Stubborn sprite! I tried another tack. "It's important for a writer to see the world," I said.

"Voyeur."

"Parking regulations penalize the poor."

"Masochist."

"It isn't fair!" I shouted.

"Fool," she said.

County Jail
December 14

Dear Lily:

I wonder if I might call upon your good graces one last time. If successful, the assistance you render could hie me out of your life forever. Surely that is a small price to pay for the opportunity to grow old with dignity.

Dear Lily, I am going through a lot of changes. What I need is a new lease on life — preferably one with a clause that allows for extensive alterations. Will you negotiate this for me?

Actually, the real reason I'm writing is to inform you that I plan to keep my nose clean for a while. More than that, I plan to apply myself to some enterprise that will make me some money and help some people, instead of just getting me in trouble. What would you think of my becoming an amateur Orthopedic Surgeon? In my experience, most people are dying for alternatives to high doctor bills.

By the way, I want to thank you for taking such good care of me over the years. I'm especially grateful to you for visiting me in jail; despite my disappointment that you didn't bring a cake or ladder, your presence made me feel a whole lot safer.

In the past week I've come to realize that the subversive influence of those who work within the system to undercut the brutality of so-called "Justice" is very great indeed. I'm sure Judge Collins would have imposed a much stiffer sentence had it not been for your intercession and your obvious concern for my well-being.

If you see my parents when you're in New York, please greet them for me. I almost feel mellow toward them today, even though I know there's not much chance of us ever being close. If I start psyching myself up now, I might be able to go east next fall for their 45th wedding anniversary – well, maybe their 50th.

I'll stop by your office one afternoon this week to see you. In fact, I want to volunteer some time to help you reorganize your law library. Please let me do that – will you?

Fondly,

Bernice

☞ JOURNAL ENTRY by Bernice Balconey

County Jail
December 15

Dear Diary:

At noon tomorrow when the prison gates clang open, I will step forth into the crisp autumn smog a free woman. Now, as the palaver subsides into sleep and snoring, I am thrown back on myself to ponder what has happened. It is a time for sobriety and reflection.

I ask myself the following questions: What next? Will I adjust to life on the Outside, or have I become hopelessly dependent on prison as a kind of security blanket? Will my friends pretend not to recognize me? Will I be able to get a job? Do I want one? What's it all about? Why me? Is there life after death? And most important, will they give me the new suit of clothes I demanded?

Perhaps it is also appropriate to consider what, if anything, I have learned from this experience. Surely I didn't need prison to find out Crime Doesn't Pay. I've known that ever since Barry Shingles said you could get free bubble gum by sticking it in your pocket instead of showing it to the check-out lady. And in sixth grade Henry David Thoreau taught me you can lead a transcendentalist to jail but you can't make him stop thinking – the poor, masochistic wretch!

I guess if there's one thing I've discovered it's that most of life's trials have absolutely no meaning. Judge Collins never listened to a word I said.

But really, there's something else I've learned, and that's how many friends I have. Most everybody from the choir came to visit me, and Rowena and Nora each came a number of times. Why is that so shocking to me? Why do I always feel so all alone?

I'm starting to realize that just because I don't get into fights with Rowena and Nora, just because they like me pretty much the way I am, doesn't make them bad people. Just because they are loyal to me doesn't mean there's something wrong with them. Perhaps arguing and trying to change another person are not prerequisites to loving. Perhaps I have been missing something.

And then there's Aurelia Sipes, who has been trying to let me down gently for more than six months. Why did I cling to her? Was it because she knew my secret – namely, that for all my railing against authority I can be pretty dictatorial myself? Was it because I didn't want to be exposed again?

Well, tonight that seems ridiculous. Am I really so hard to love? Rowena and Nora both say no. They want me to go on a trip with them to Mexico. I may just do it, too, if I can scrape up some money fast.

Miraculously, I am filled with energy to make something of my life. I feel like expanding out of every shell — shyness, good manners, social conventions, inhibition, the bounds of taste, this body, limitations of my brain, the nuclear family, coupleism, the confines of this 10-by-12-bit room, and, better still, my name. These silly boundaries, these walls and bars, these rules I will not harken to (or anyway, not yet — I'm much too young to hang it up).

So what will I do next? I think that I will find some way to live, instead of merely playing at it. Or perhaps I'll do what Aurelia says is wrong: i.e., try to impose my "weird sense of disorder on the world." (Isn't that what writing is about?)

Meanwhile, I will have to find a way to make some money. I suppose that for a while at least that might mean taking a real job.

What do you say, dear diary?

Should I wing it, instead?

December 16

Dearest Aurelia:

Can you guess where I am writing from? The airport! No, I am not about to take a trip. I am merely reveling in the illusion that travel is possible. Nora Bleeble thinks I am flying already, keeps pestering me for a confession that jail has made a junkie out of me. In truth, I am elated to have re-discovered liberty of movement; if I am tripping it is only the air I stumble on.

Nora picked me up at noon. After gorging ourselves on all the tacos, pizza, and egg-rolls three dollars would buy (about half a swallow each), we put in cameo appearances at the bus depot and train station, then hightailed it out here to the airport. I have been sitting by the window for hours, watching the big birds come and go. Who cares if it is done with mirrors — the spectacle is dazzling nonetheless.

Oh, Aurelia, my life is definitely picking up. I'm sure it's got something to do with being done with jail, but that's not all. So many things seem so much clearer. For example, I finally understand that you are staying in New Hampshire, and that your trip home at Christmas is just to wrap things up. Am I right? Actually, I'm pretty sure you've been trying to tell me that for months, but I wouldn't let you. I didn't want to hear it. Well, now I'm ready.

I will, of course, pick you up at the airport on December 23, as per our earlier arrangement. Please be informed that I have been practicing pride and self-respect on Nora and Rowena; with any luck, I won't spend all the time on my knees begging for another chance. In fact, I think you'll find me happier than I've been in months.

Yours with repressed passion,

Bernice Balconey
Aspiring Cucumber

P.S. I forgot to tell you: in a few days our choir is giving a concert in the supply cabinet of the Women's Coalition. Mind you, that isn't the space we requested, but it was all we were able to get. I sincerely hope that no one interprets our failure to book the bathtub as a commentary on the quality of our music.
. . .We'll be singing a medley of old Solstice favorites: "Noisy Night, Pagan Night," "O Little Town of Milwaukee," "Gloria in Excelsis Steinem," "It's My Party And I'll Cry If I Want To" and many more. Too bad you won't be back in time to join the festivities.
P.P.S. If I throw up bridges that are wobbly and in bad locations, I hope you will at least trust in the love that panics there. I want us to be friends, okay?

B.B.B.
Bridge-Building Beginner

☞ LILY BARNSTRAW TO BERNICE BALCONEY

December 21

My dear Bernice:

When I arrived at my office this morning, it was with considerable shock that I noted the changes in my law library. As I recall, our "contract" provided that the two of us would work together for three or four Saturdays to complete the reorganization. I certainly would not have given you a key had I known that you would finish the job over the course of a single weekend. It was never my intention to let you do all that work by yourself.

In truth, Bernice, I must admit that you did a commendable job, and that I am quite pleased with the results. My only regret, in fact, is that I let you convince me to agree never to mention payment – you certainly deserve to be compensated for your efforts. If you had not reiterated the point in the note you left with those lovely roses, I would have enclosed a check with this letter and begged you to reconsider. Instead, I will merely state that I wish you would change your mind, and that in my view I owe you some money.

Bernice, since you and I have not discussed your behavior in court on December 7, there are a couple of comments I feel compelled to make. First, as you no doubt realize by now, your coming to court dressed as Justice was no insurance that Justice would be done. Although you did a surprisingly tasteful job of arranging the folds of the white sheet you draped around your body, the rest of your costume was hardly calculated to endear you to Judge Collins. In particular, I am referring to the "blindfold" you wore at a rakish angle covering only part of one eye, and the scales you carried, weighted down on one side with coins and dollars. I personally was not offended by your wielding a huge gavel instead of the traditional two-edged sword, but when you started banging it on the table to emphasize your points, I wished that I had had the foresight to deposit it in the umbrella rack outside the court.

The second point I wish to make is a bit more positive. Bernice, I must confess that when Judge Collins asked you if you had any final comments, I was extremely anxious that you would do or say something offensive. Instead, you launched into a well-thought-out, articulate attack on the city of Milwaukee's night parking regulations. Had I understood earlier that you entertained such principled objections to the discriminatory impact of those laws, I might have been more sympathetic to your protest. Obviously, judging from the murmurs of approval from the other people in the courtroom, your speech struck a responsive chord.

Nevertheless, Bernice, there is one aspect of your character that I suppose I will never undertand, and that is why you almost invariably get carried away. What started out as a rational, orderly exposure of injustice eventually deteriorated – apparently in proportion to the crowd's approval – to a rambling, semi-incoherent tirade punctuated by raps of your gavel on the table in front of you. When Judge Collins threatened to jail you for contempt of court and you shouted "Give me Liberty or Give me Contempt," I knew it was all over. The rest of the scenario I need not repeat.

Fortunately, you seem to have made the most of your experience in jail, and to have survived it with your irrepressible good humor – which I do admire, Bernice, even though I think you sometimes go too far – intact. In particular, it is gratifying to me that you now appear to understand a little more fully the complexities and contradictions of my role. On my side, I can honestly state that I learned some important lessons from you, not the least of them being to laugh occasionally at the absurdities my role also presents. Bernice, thank you for the work you did, and for the roses. I sincerely hope that we are able to maintain our friendship in the future.

Affectionately,

Lily

☞ BERNICE BALCONEY TO THE AUTHOR

May 5

Dear Georgia:

Now that you've read all the letters, I think I should tell you what happened. I was right about Aurelia: she was hopelessly in love with Jenny Fribbenz and could hardly wait to get back to New Hampshire. Still, we had a few good talks and made a satisfactory settlement regarding the stuff of hers I pawned. In truth, after the shock wore off, I think she was grateful not to have to move it. We're still in touch by letter.

I did go travelling with Nora and Rowena. They threw a benefit for me the night I got out of jail, and the money raised was just enough to pay my share of expenses. We had a fantastic time, even though we only made it as far as New Orleans. We toyed briefly with the idea of buying a boat, painting it lavender, and going into shrimping, but, like most of our plans, this one went up in marijuana.

On a more serious note, I've been doing some investigative work for Lily Barnstraw. She's handling more criminal cases these days and sometimes calls me in to locate and interview witnesses. In fact, she's now representing two of the women I met in jail, which makes me a lot less anxious about their cases. I'm pleased to stay in touch with them.

Incredibly, I continue to be filled with ambition. Perhaps it was having that Contempt-of-Court label stuck on me that gave me a sense of direction. I regard it as a sort of merit badge. Now that it's earned I am content — nay, grateful — to move on to a new challenge, although, of course, I will display this one proudly on my sash.

So what will I tackle next? Well, I think I'll go for the merit badge in Filthy Lucre: how to get it, how to spend it. That's where you come in. I'm hoping that the letters you just read will appeal to a few skeptics like myself, or, better yet, to the misguided many who take perverted pleasure in reading other people's mail.

Actually, my goal is for the book to bring in enough money to finance the Broadway musical, and then the movie. After that, there's sure to be a television series. I've even started my own production company. Nora and Rowena are working with me on it.

We've already got a couple of projects going. One is a cinéma vérité exposé of judicial corruption, which we call Traffic Court. The plan is to set up cameras in Judge Collins' courtroom and follow the action for a couple days. Eventually we may even be able to buy some film! The other project is a lively, light-hearted,

optimistic soap opera about the efforts of a group of
women to overcome jealousy and possessiveness in
their lives. So far the best title we've come up with is
Less Miserable, but that doesn't quite capture the
hopefulness we're after. Any ideas?

As you can see, I've given up feeling sorry for
myself and am now in the process of translating my
misfortunes into gain. I suppose some would call
that "growing up," but we know that's absurd. I prefer
to think of it as "wising up" — by far the better term
for women with smart mouths. (That's me!) I'm on
my way...

Expectantly,

Bernice

P.S. What do you think about including the following
tear-off sheet at the end of the book:

YES! I think it is a crime for an artiste like
Bernice Balconey to have to work at a regular job.
Enroll me in the Society for the Preservation of
Bernice Balconey's Psychic Freedom. I enclose my
check or money order (payable to Georgia Ressmeyer,
c/o Metis Press, P.O. Box 25187, Chicago IL 60625) in
the amount of $ _____ .

Signed,

_____
Your name goes here.

Photo by Lauren Whitney Holmes

GEORGIA JO RESSMEYER was born in 1947 and grew up in a parsonage on Long Island. She has also lived in Indiana, Chicago, Tokyo, New Haven, and Milwaukee. Besides writing, her careers have included shearing Christmas trees, teaching English as a second language, practicing law, and organizing women. She likes writing best. She loves women. Her sexual preference is the Midwest.

Thanks to the incomparable team that finally got *Bernice* between covers:

Joyce Bolinger
Dolores Connelly
Pam Graves
Lynn Hull
Chris Johnson
Chris Straayer

Pat Kludka
Marie Kuda
Nancy Poore
Georgia Jo
 Ressmeyer
Mona Straayer

Thanks also to Woodland Pattern Book Center and to Janet Soule.

...Ernestine, a fast little press, and her granny letterpress Pearl.

Bookbinding by A Fine Bind / Iowa City Women's Press

Other books by Metis Press:

Hurtin' & Healin' & Talkin' It Over, by Arny Christine Straayer

Wild Women Don't Get the Blues, by Barbara Emrys

Shedevils, by Barbara Sheen

A Book of One's Own; Guide to Self-Publishing, by Chris Johnson & Chris Straayer

The Secret Witch, by Linda Johnson Stem

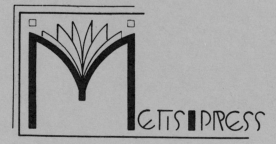

METIS PRESS

P.O. BOX 25187 ■ CHICAGO, ILLINOIS 60625

The book you are holding is hand made.

Metis Press is a woman owned and operated print shop and publisher. We are dedicated to the fine crafts of bookmaking, from typography and design through printing and binding. The difference in this personal interest is comparable to that of hand made fabrics or jewelry as contrasted with the department store variety. Such hand crafts are special in a way that makes you want to give them to friends.

This book is the product of a commitment and attitude rather than of modern printing technology. If it looks slick it is because our skill and patience were able to coax results out of our equipment — and we are proud of that. To some people, a handcrafted book may mean only an expensive hardback, sewn together and bound in silk or morocco for a collector. To us it also means a high-quality paperback edition of fine writing, beautifully made from materials and methods that keep it accessible to a deservedly wide audience. As we put it together, we like to think that each copy will go to a friend.